Knowing You

CAMILE R. RIGBY

REX RIAN

To my wonderful Mom
Thanks for your love and instilling in me a
passion for books and reading.
Miss you.

Chapter 1

May 1987, Rocky Mountains, USA

It was like watching a silent, black and white movie someone had torn apart, bits and pieces; images and feelings careening randomly through my mind.

Warm sand coated the bottom of my bare feet. Waves crawled on the shore, tinting the sand as they glided away. The shadow of a bird moved past me before disappearing into obscurity.

The tight grip on my hand was almost painful, the dirt and moist leaves cool to the soles of my feet. Whoever held me urged me quickly on towards the sound of rushing water. Adrenalin flew through my veins. The ground disappeared from beneath my feet and I landed in the middle of my bedroom back home.

The sound of girls' chatter outside my door, plucked me from my dream. I opened my eyes, stretched and looked around. This wasn't my bedroom. I was lying in an old metal bed, one of two in the room. Two gray metal cabinets stood by the far wall leaving my clothes for all to see, a naked light bulb hung suspended from the ceiling. A square window sported a broken blind that only let in strips of the early morning sun. The walls were a painted white but after years of neglect, looked more like a blending of yellows and grays.

I had just spent my first night away from home. A nervous but excited flutter filled my stomach. Leaving home had been a hard choice to make. Mom had only been gone a few years and I knew dad could have used my help this summer but I wanted to get away. Glancing at the picture frame on the small black dresser by my bed I studied the likeness of myself standing by mom a few months before the cancer took her. Our hair blended together as we hugged close in the photo, mine thick and dark and hers so very thin. Her blue eyes were not so bright. I could see the forced smile on my face.

Closing my eyes, I lay back and thought of the room I shared with my sister, Esther; the room where I first had the dream. The pale lemon walls and breezy white curtains Mom had picked out for us covered the large window. Rainbows of sunlight reflected off the rummage-sale chandelier as pale pinks, greens and blues splashed across the old grey hope chest that cradled all my childhood treasures.

Fumbling, I reached into my backpack sitting on the floor next to the bed and slid a brown leather journal out of the center pocket. The corners were worn dull and smooth with use, and pages were beginning to separate from the binding. Sitting up I tucked my pillow behind my back, found a page with some space and began to write.

A line of blue ink gashed my page as my hand jerked, ripping me again from my dream. Reaching over I smacked off the alarm and threw back the covers, leaving my journal for another time. Slipping my feet in my flip-flops I snatched my bag of toiletries and clean clothes and left my room.

The khaki pants of my uniform fit well on my curvy figure. The dark green shirt almost matched the green of my eyes where a trace of sadness lingered. I carefully brushed the tangles from my long brown hair, chose a hair scrunchy out of my bag and slid it onto my wrist. It didn't take long to gather my things and drop them off in my room as I headed off to breakfast.

The employee cafeteria was teeming with people. I hurried over to the buffet and stared at the food. My stomach growled as I considered the mountains of pastries, sausage, eggs, pancakes, toast, granola and yogurt that sat before me just waiting to be chosen. I was happy that I didn't have to eat cracked wheat cereal again; the breakfast of choice according to my dad. That was like him, he wore the same kind of pants every day and always requested the same aftershave for birthdays or Christmas.

I settled on a stack of fluffy pancakes and poured on maple syrup until they seemed to float. I took a glass of juice and with a deep breath began to make my way through the maze of tables and chairs. An empty chair near one of the windows seemed to call to me. Smiling a little at the other occupants of the table I sank into the seat and set my tray down.

The mountains beyond the resort were covered with an array of pine and quaking aspen trees. The granite rocks jutted up through the clouds. I was mesmerized as I watched a moose swim at the edge of the small lake.

"Hey," a voice broke in, drawing me out of the scene before me. "Could you do me a favor?"

I looked up to see a pretty, light brown-haired girl with bright blue eyes. She wore the same green and khaki uniform, and in her hand she held an incredibly large muffin. "I grabbed this muffin off the buffet, but there's no way that I'll be able to finish it by myself. Will you take half?" she smiled expectantly. "They're really good, I promise," she affirmed, noting my hesitation.

"Um...ok. Thanks," I smiled shyly as the girl sat down across from me.

"I'm Kennedy," she began, tearing the muffin in half, "but everyone calls me Kenny."

"I'm Vivian," I replied, accepting the blueberry muffin from Kenny's outstretched hand.

"I haven't seen you around before. Did you just get here?" Kenny asked, popping a bite of muffin into her mouth.

"Yeah. Just last night. It was kind of weird having the room all to myself," I explained, "I was expecting to have a roommate."

"Oh, you'll have a roommate," Kenny assured. "At least one; the rooms always fill up by the end of the first week. There's so much staff here." Kenny looked toward the door. "Oh, there are some of my friends. I'm meeting up with them for breakfast." She smiled again. "Want to come sit with us?"

I held in a sigh of relief. "Sure, thanks," I replied as I set the muffin on my tray and followed Kenny across the room, grateful that she had approached me. Maybe making new friends would be easier than I thought.

"Rochelle, Tammy, this is Vivian; she just got here last night," Kenny said.

As we settled into our seats I smiled at the two girls on the other side of the table.

"Where are you working?" Tammy asked.

Turning to her I could see she was a cute girl with forest green eyes. The dark makeup she wore contrasted with her short, curly blond hair.

"Housekeeping," I said. "What exactly do we do?" I asked as I picked up the muffin and took a bite.

Tammy answered first. "Cleaning," she said, "And cleaning and cleaning and cleaning." She bobbed her head from side to side as she spoke, making her blond curly hair swish across her face.

"It's not gonna be that bad, Tammy. We're all cleaning. It's not like spending the summer on the beach, but it's easy and we get paid for it," Rochelle said as she pushed her black, wool hat out of her eyes.

"That's why I come here," Kenny said pointing out the window. "Look at those mountains. They're amazing!"

Rochelle looked down at her watch. "Oh, guys, we should get going. Orientation starts in a few minutes."

"We better stop chatting and get eating," Kenny said.

We made short work of our food, picked up our trays and headed for the door.

"Where is Kimi?" Tammy asked, emptying her tray into the trash can. "She's going to be late, again."

"That girl," Kenny said affectionately. "She's never been on time to anything in her life."

"No, but she sure knows how to have a good time," Rochelle replied. "Just wait til you meet Kimi, Vivian. You'll love her."

Glad to have some new friends; I followed them down the long hallways of the resort to the conference room. The large room was already filling up with men and women of all ages. We found a row of empty seats near the front and sat down.

"This usually doesn't take very long," Rochelle said.

"If there aren't any questions let's break into groups and give you a tour of our hotel," said the young man doing the orientation.

It began in the lobby, as we ascended the grand staircase we were presented with an imposing display of the mountains before us, framed by large picture windows. A large fireplace sat against one wall, a cheery fire warming the room. Couches, chairs and end tables seemed to comfortably fill the large space.

"This is my favorite room in the resort," Rochelle said.

Leaving the lounge we passed the 4 star restaurant and moved out the nearby door to a stone covered patio. A set of stairs dropped down to a nearby path which meandered through the pines and opened up to a stunning garden with a spacious swimming pool and hot tub.

Exiting the garden we headed back inside. After passing the administrative offices we continued down the hall to the laundry. Waiting inside was a short, slightly plump woman of South American descent. Her black hair hung in a cute bob that settled just above the green polo she wore.

She smiled as we filed into the room.

"Hi, my name is Sylvia; I'm in charge of the laundry and housekeeping. I've been here for 15 years," she said, her accent obvious as she spoke.

She explained our duties and gave us our cart and room assignments and then demonstrated how to fold the towel swans. After creating four swans she gave us a paper with directions and sent us out to work.

"The service elevator is just around the corner," she said as we began exiting the laundry, "for you who are working on levels two and three."

I just stared at the list and swan directions for a moment as I walked to my cart

"Um, Kenny," I whispered as we walked down the hall pushing our carts laden with towels and cleaning supplies, "I don't know if I can get all these rooms done. I'll be here all night."

"You're gonna do great, Vivian," Kenny said. "Trust me; you'll catch on much quicker than you think." She put a hand on my shoulder before turning into a guest room. Only half believing her, I walked nervously down the hallway. 100, I thought. Start with room 100 and work your way to the front.

My work was slow, but steady, as I went through each room putting clean linens on the beds, placing mints on pillows and room service menus on dressers, and arranging towels in the bathrooms. Because it was my first day, I'd been given a cart full of towels already intricately folded to look like swans, but soon I would be expected to do it myself.

By three o'clock, I had made it through over half of the rooms on my list. It had gone better than I expected, but I knew that I certainly wasn't as fast as Kenny and the other girls. I was doing my best to hurry when a young woman blew into the room like a whirlwind. She wore the same tidy uniform, but her hair was a chaotic, curly mess, and her cheeks were flushed pink.

"Oh sorry!" she giggled. "I thought I was supposed to start at 100. But it must be 10." Despite her disorderly appearance I liked her instantly. "I'm Kimi," she said, smiling.

"Oh, hi," I said. "Some of the other girls were wondering where you   were   this   morning."

"Tammy, Rochelle, and Kenny, right?" she said.

I nodded.

"Those girls are always worrying about me. I got lost and ran out of gas. You'd think I would know how to get here after two summers," she shook her head and smiled. "Well, I guess I should get to 10. I don't have a whole lot of time to get it all done."

"Good luck!" I answered. "

"Oh no worries! I'm a pro," Kimi said and turned to leave. "It was nice meeting you...what's your name?"

"Vivian."

"Well, it was nice meeting you Vivian. I'll see you around," she said as she hurried out the door.

I smiled as I neatly arranged the towels and put out a fresh bar of soap.

"Hey Vivian!" Kimi's voice sounded, making me jump. As I turned around, I could see her tight curls bounce as she peeked around the doorway.

"Yeah?"

"I'd probably get a talking to if one of the supervisors saw me with my hair like this," she grinned. "You wouldn't happen to have a scrunchie I could borrow, would you?"

I smiled and tossed her the one on my wrist.

A few hours later I was glad to be checking off the last room on my list. It had been a long busy day but I was pleased with what I had accomplished. Given a couple more days and I would have the swan thing down as well.

Later that night, I wandered into the cafeteria comfortable in my well-worn pair of light-washed jeans and blue t-shirt that my mom had given me. Rochelle waved me over to the buffet, where chafing dishes full of steaming roast beef and perfectly smooth mashed potatoes were waiting for us. As I loaded up my plate, and topped it with a golden-brown buttered roll, I realized how hungry I was. As soon as we joined the other girls at their window-side table, I dug into my dinner.

"So, Vivian, how did your first day go?" Kenny asked excitedly.

I swallowed a mouthful of potatoes. "It wasn't too bad," I answered.

"I started out a little slow but the work got easier as I went along. I think I will be fine once I figure out the swan thing.

Rochelle and Tammy laughed.

"It took me weeks to figure that out!" Rochelle said. "But eventually you get it."

"Yeah, and until then there's always someone nearby who will try to help you," Tammy added.

"Have you got a roommate yet?" Rochelle asked as we went back to eating.

"No, maybe tomorrow," I said.

"I don't have a roommate either, let's stop by personnel after dinner and see if I can switch rooms," she said.

"I'd like that, thanks," I smiled

"Hey Kenny!" A deep voice broke in. Vivian looked over and saw a tall good-looking guy across the dining room. "Volleyball tonight? You girls in?"

Kenny looked around the table as everyone nodded. "Yeah, we're in," she called back to him.

He raised both thumbs, a grin on his face. "Cool!" He turned and jogged out the door, slapping a short, dark haired guy on the back as he went.

We had all taken our positions in the sand, ready to start the game. I was poised in the back right corner of the court, prepared to dive for the ball if the guys attempted to hit it out of our reach. My hair was pulled up in a ponytail. To my left, stood a tall, slender girl.

"I'm Jackie," she said, waiting for the game to start. "Jackie McKinnon."

I smiled and dug my toes into the sand. "I'm Vivian. Are you on the cleaning staff too?" I asked.

"No, I'm a waitress. I work in the café and restaurant. Tammy and Kimi used to be over there too, before they switched."

"They switched?" I said a little surprised. "I figured waitressing was better than cleaning."

"Well, it is except for the hours. We're up at dawn and don't go down til after 10. But cleaning, once you're done with your rooms, you're done for the day," Jackie clarified.

"Oh, I see."

"Hey, do you know where Rochelle is? She usually loves volleyball," Jackie said.

"I think she's back in our room. She said something about doing some drawing..."

"Oh, okay. She's an artist, going to school for it and everything. These mountains are probably too good to resist, you know?"

She was interrupted by Tony's California slur.

"If you girls are done chatting, we can get started."

"You in a hurry to lose?" Tammy taunted.

"Oh you think—"Tony began, but he was interrupted by the guy standing next to him.

"Just stop flirting and serve the ball, Anthony," he teased. He was of average height and weight, had pleasant features and stylish brown hair. Tony rolled his eyes, and tossed the ball into the air. It made contact with his fist and rocketed over the net.

Kenny slid to her knees and sent it high, it gave me time to get under the ball and spike it to the other side. The ball landed in the sand next to grass, it was tossed back under the net to Jackie who set up for an underhand serve. It barely made it over the net and Tony easily returned it. The volley continued for a few minutes until Kyle launched the ball, causing sand to scatter as it skidded to a stop under Tammy's foot.

Tammy's serve went wild, ricocheted off the pole and flew out of bounds.

"Do over," she called.

The ball was sent back and her next serve bounced off Kyle's arms, setting up a spike for Tony. Jumping in his face I blocked it and it fell to the ground at his feet.

A broad grin spread across my face. I loved volleyball. I loved the power and control I had over the ball.

That cute guy's serve came next. He sent it right at me. That's how I started thinking of him, "the cute guy". I stepped back and attacked the ball, hurled it over the net, right past him. He landed on his back in an effort to return it.

My turn to serve, I threw the ball high; my hand connected and sent the ball speeding towards the net, skimming the top as it went over. Tony had gotten a mouthful of sand as his tall, muscular form dove for the ball. It hit the ground and rolled off into the grass.

"Way to wipe the smile off Tony's face, Viv!" Kenny said victoriously.

The high pitched call of birds was our only warning. A small flock shot past, narrowly missing our heads and the net.

"That was crazy," Jackie said.

The bounce of the net caught my eye. A small bird had its long wings tangled. It became more entrapped as it frantically tried to free itself.

Kyle slowly walked up and stood quietly in front it, as if trying to communicate. Trapped under the weight of its own wings the bird began to tire. Kyle's hand stretched out slowly to touch the bird, the thrashing of panicked wings stopped him.He just stood there unmoving.

"Just relax and calm down, it will be ok," I heard myself whisper.

As if it listened to me, the bird stopped, visibly shaking as it hung from the trap it had made.

Carefully, with Kyle's help, the strings fell away releasing its captive. We watched as it flew off into the pink and orange sunset to freedom.

Everyone else was still huddled around the net talking about the bird, when I wandered to the edge of the court and sat down. The grass felt cool against my bare legs.

"The cute guy" caught my eye and winked. I felt my lips curl up in response. He left the group, strolled over and sat down. His long legs stretched out in front, ankles crossed.

"That was an interesting ending to the game," he said nodding towards the net.

"Ya, that was pretty weird," I said.

I sat there searching for something intelligent to say.

"You're good," he said, nudging my shoulder.

"Um...thanks," I said. I was suddenly conscious of my unruly hair and the ten—or fifteen—pounds that I wanted to lose.

"I'm Jeff," he said. "And you are?"

"Vivian," I answered. Finally, a name to put with "the cute guy".

He smiled warmly, and his kind brown eyes reminded me of my brother's.

"Did you play volleyball in high school or something?" Jeff asked.

"Yeah. All four years."

"Cool! I played too, but only for one year. I got into basketball junior and senior year and my parents said I could only do one."

"I love basketball!" I said. "But I've always been better at watching it than actually playing it."

"That's how I am with football. Love it, but I've never been very good at it." I nodded my head, not sure what to say next. Luckily, Jeff wasn't about to allow an awkward silence. "Do you want to go grab a drink?" he asked, gesturing to the cooler next to court.

"Yeah, sounds great," I answered. I walked with him toward the cooler, keeping a half a step behind him as we went.

"So, does your family like sports? It's a tradition for mine."

"Well, not all of us play, but my dad was a basketball star in college, so we all watch," I said.

"Oh yeah? Where did he play?"

Soon we had our drinks and I found myself telling Jeff all about my dad's college days, and how he and my mother met. He listened intently more and more reminding me of my older brother, Mark.

Finally, I ran out of things to say, and we sat quietly in the grass next to the volleyball court.

"It's nice to have someone new around," Jeff remarked. "The other girls are great, but they can be a bit...silly sometimes," he said, nodding to Kimi and Tammy. They were running around on the grass, trying to empty water bottles onto each other.

I laughed as I watched them run. "I guess. But they know how to have fun."

"You seem a little quieter; I like that in a girl."

A nervous flutter filled me, and I silently hoped that the conversation would go where I thought it was heading.

"Hey, do you want to go out with me sometime?" he asked, just as I had supposed. "The restaurant here is actually really good. How about Friday night?"

"That sounds nice," I said.

"Cool," Jeff said smiling excitedly. "I'll meet you in the lobby at six, see you around."

"See you," I said as he walked away. I looked up at the sky, just dark enough that the stars were starting to dot the velvety blue. I waved goodbye to Jackie and the others and wandered back to my room. New friends and now a date, I was beginning to really like this summer.

Chapter 2

The lobby wasn't very crowded when I arrived for my date with Jeff. I couldn't see him so I looked around for a place to sit. There was a family with 3 young children trying to check in. One little boy with curly blond hair kept running up and down the grand staircase. I wondered if he always had that much energy or if it was the result of being cooped up in a car all day. I moved to a small grouping of wingback chairs that were tucked next to the stairs and sat down to wait.

He came sauntering in 15 minutes later wearing a ratty t-shirt, board shorts and flip flops. I looked down at my pink, cap sleeved blouse, tan pants and white ballet flats.

"You ready to eat?" he asked walking up.

"Sure," I said standing up.

In just a few minutes we were seated at a small table in the middle of the room. Jeff's eyes lit up as he looked at me. The smile on my face froze when I realized he was looking past me, at the waitress who had come up. I took the menu she offered with a quiet thank you.

Glancing through the menu I was a little shocked at the prices. I had never eaten in such a nice place before. I wasn't sure what to get. I finally decided on a chicken dish that sounded enticing. The waitress returned with our drinks and took our order. I noticed Jeff watching her as she walked away.

My dinner turned out to be a grilled chicken breast topped with a mushroom sauce and roasted vegetables on the side. The blending of flavors was like a kaleidoscope of colors to my mouth. Jeff got a very rare steak and baked potato.

We talked about life before that summer, what we were studying in school, the usual first date questions. I kept noticing Jeff look around the room as if I were boring him. After this happened 3 or 4 times I realized that every time he did, a waitress would walk by.

I didn't say too much after that, just let Jeff do the talking, which he was happy to do. I've never heard a guy talk so much about themselves. I just wanted this evening to be over.

Jeff finally waved the waitress over and she returned a few minutes later with our bills, as in plural. Surprised and a little offended, I pulled some money out of my wallet and paid for my meal, which ended up being the highlight of the evening.

Jeff insisted on walking me back to my room. I felt his hand brush mine as we walked. I quickly folded my arms and kept them there. No way was I going to hold hands with this jerk. I told Jeff goodbye as we walked up to my door and hurried inside to the safety of my room.

The next morning arrived too soon. I tossed and turned most of the night worried about how I could keep away from Jeff.

"See you at breakfast," Rochelle said as she left the room. I looked up from where I was tying my shoes to see her walk back in the room.

"Jeff's on his way down the hall," she whispered. "Good luck."

And with that my roommate left me to deal with him.

I didn't want to talk to him and wasn't too happy about our date. I was hoping to avoid him for a couple of days. But there he was standing outside my door. He told me he had a wonderful time. That didn't surprise me. I cringed every time I thought about it. I was feeling antsy as Jeff kept going on and on. My ears tuning him out as I thought of all the things I could be doing, like getting breakfast.

"I've got to go or I'll be late for work," I cut in. The door clicked shut and I started down the hall, Jeff trailing along behind me.

"I'll see you later Viv!" I heard him call after me as I hurried away. I winced, hating the way he thought he knew me well enough to call me that.

When I finally made it to my first room, I was out of breath and red-cheeked. I flung fresh sheets onto the bed and vigorously smoothed out the wrinkles. I vacuumed, dusted, and tidied. Then, I moved onto the bathroom, taking out my frustration on the grout between the shower tiles. I scrubbed so hard that by the time I was done, my face was even redder and my arms ached with the effort. Despite my exhaustion, I was starting to feel a bit better. But then I saw a stack of towels folded neatly into squares sitting on the counter. My heart sunk as I remembered that starting today, I would have to somehow turn that neat stack of towels into four graceful swans. It seemed that that morning, no task had ever looked so daunting.

Hesitantly, I approached the first towel. I folded carefully, matching up edges and making sure to define each crease. I did everything exactly as it described on the paper I had been given, or so I thought. But when I finished, it looked more like a melted snowman than a swan.

So much for step by step directions, I thought looking at the mess I had made. Reaching for another towel I tried again. This one turned out only slightly better. I knew I shouldn't get frustrated over a little towel but that and the crappy date with Jeff had left me with a crummy attitude. Determined to try again I picked up the last towel and began to fold. As I watched, the towel slowly came unfolded.

That was it. I just couldn't take it anymore. Seizing the towel I threw it out the door towards my cart.

"You okay Vivian?" I heard Kenny call from across the hall.

I flushed red. "Yeah, I'm okay."

"You sure about that?" she said walking into my room. "Cuz either that towel was trying to kill you, or something is wrong." Kenny raised an eyebrow.

"It's these towels, I have tried 3 times and I can't get it too work." Between that and Jeff, I'm just a little frustrated.

"Okay, listen. I'll help you out," Kenny began. "This is how I learned to do the towels." She retrieved a clean towel from the stack and laid it out on the counter. "You match up these two edges, pull up here, fold these corners up, and tuck this part in. Then, you flip it over and fold this part over and...voila!" It had taken her less than a minute to produce a perfectly folded towel.

"That's exactly what I thought I did," I said.

"How about this," Kenny said. "Grab your towels and I'll get mine and we'll fold all of them now. You should get it after doing that many."

"That sounds perfect," I said as we went into the hall to get the towels.

Thirty minutes and a bed full of beautiful, swan towels later I shut the door and Kenny and I left for lunch.

"So, what's going on with Jeff?" Kenny said mischievously, as we walked down the sidewalk to the cafeteria. "What'd he do to ruffle your feathers this morning?"

"Nothing much," I sighed. "He just thinks our date went better than it actually did."

"Uh-oh. No second date, then?" she concluded.

"No way. Even running into him at work is too much."

"Viv, he's one of the hottest guys here," Kenny said sarcastically. "Like, have you seen his eyes?"

I laughed. "Yeah, I've seen his eyes," I said, "while they were checking out every waitress in the restaurant."

Kenny made a disgusted face. "Seriously? What a jerk." We were still smiling when we reached the cafeteria.

"Yeah. I got all dressed up, and he showed up in flip-flops. Flip flops! And, he made me pay for half," I added.

"That's just downright rude. If he asks, he pays, that's how it works."

"Well apparently, he didn't get the memo."

"Just tell me you didn't let him kiss you," Kenny said seriously. "It seems like that's all he wanted, a little make-out session."

"He tried, but no. I just left him standing outside my door," I assured her.

We glanced around the cafeteria as we walked in and saw Kimi at a table by the window, waving impatiently at us. "Hold your horses!" Kenny called. We stepped quickly into line behind a couple of lifeguards.

"Don't look now," Kenny whispered grinning, "but Jeff is eyeing you big time."

"That's not funny," I said, though I was stifling a laugh myself. I took a sidelong glance at the nearest group of tables and, sure enough, Jeff was looking in my direction with a perpetual smile on his face. I snapped my eyes forward. "Kenny, what am I gonna do?" I said. "I can't take this all summer, but how do I tell him it's not happening?"

"We'll figure something out," Kenny comforted. "But for now, let's just get some sandwiches, and we'll tell the other girls we're gonna eat outside. That way, at least, you can eat without him staring at you the whole time."

"Okay," I breathed. At last we were at the front of the line, just far enough away that Jeff couldn't look at me without turning around in his chair. Even he wasn't indiscreet enough to do that.

"You're kidding me?" Kenny moaned. "All the sandwiches are gone."

"I guess we'll have to eat..."

"Come on," she interrupted, grabbing my arm and pulling me with her. "There has got to be more in the kitchen."

"Are you sure we're allowed in there?" I asked.

"Just come on. The sooner we get some sandwiches, the sooner we get out of here."

I let her drag me along, if only to get me farther from Jeff's puppy-dog gaze and closer to a good meal.

"Can I help you?" A small, woman wearing a brightly colored apron asked as we entered the sunny kitchen. Her dark brown hair was pulled into two thick braids that flowed down her back.

"They're all out of sandwiches out front," Kenny explained. "Do you have any more back here?"

"Oh, of course!" the woman replied. "Sorry there aren't any out. My server is out sick today so we're a bit short-handed." She opened up the industrial-sized refrigerator and stepped up onto a little stool to reach the highest shelf. With her big smile and commanding presence, I didn't realize until then just how short the woman was.

She pulled down a huge tray of sandwiches.

"Do you want some help with that?" I asked, stepping up to give her a hand.

"Oh, thank you sweetie," she replied as we set the tray on the counter. Reaching back in, she pulled out a smaller tray.

"Kenny, Vivian, come on!" Rochelle's voice broke through, her head sticking in the doorway, her lips in a pout.

"We're coming!" Kenny said, grabbing a sandwich off the tray.

"Do you want some help taking these out?" I asked the woman, not wanting to abandon her.

"That would be wonderful! Thank you!" she said cheerfully.

I picked up the smaller of the two trays.

"We'll find a table outside and save you a spot, okay?" Kenny said, already at the door.

"Okay," I answered, though I had been expecting her to offer her help as well. But now, it seemed, I would be stuck carrying the massive tray alone. As Kenny and Rochelle bounced through the kitchen door and into the dining room, I turned back to the woman. "I'm Vivian, by the way," I said. The corners of her mouth turned up in a smile, causing wrinkles to appear by her eyes.

"I'm Jessie," the woman replied. "Now," she said, "I think this other tray might be a bit heavy for you to carry. Let me find you some help." She poked her own head through the door into the dining room and called out. "Nic! Nic, come here for a minute!" A few seconds later, a tall young man sauntered into the room.

"Yes, Miss Jessie?" he said cheerfully.

He was tall and impressively chiseled. His fitted shirt outlined the smooth, rolling contours of his muscles. His eyes were blue and his smile came easily.

"I need you to take these out to the dining room, please," Jessie instructed. "Vivian will show you where they go."

"No problem," he agreed, lifting the tray. "Lead the way, mademoiselle," he said, flashing me a playful smile.

I blushed and looked down at the tray of sandwiches. I could see Jessie's smile out of the corner of my eye. I made my way to the door, and began to turn to push it open with my back but Nic beat me to it.

"After you," he said. I glanced up quickly, mumbled a thank you and scooted past him into the cafeteria.

I walked to the table and set down the tray, eager to be outside, away from Jeff's stare and Nic's beautiful smile.

"Vivian is a pretty name," he said as we unloaded our trays. "I like it."

"Thanks," I replied, somehow managing not to stutter. "Is Nic your whole name, or is it short for Nicholas?"

"It's short for Nicholas," he answered. He took my empty tray from my hands. "I'll take that back to the kitchen for you," he grinned. "It was nice to meet you, Vivian."

The deep timbre of his voice felt like velvet on my skin.

"You as well," I said as he turned to leave.

I stood at the table for a few seconds, until out of the corner of my eye, I saw Jeff stand up from his seat. I made a precipitous escape out the patio door.

"...Seriously, a shoe?" Tammy was saying as I sat down at the table. "How do you forget just one shoe?"

"Oh, that's nothing!" Rochelle began. "I found a box of diapers. Like the whole thing. Those parents are probably gonna be pretty upset when their kid has a blowout and they realize they don't have any diapers."

"Vivian!" Tammy said. "Finally! What took you so long?"

"Oh, nothing," I said. "I was just helping Jessie with some things in the kitchen." I didn't mention Nic; I wanted to keep that to myself for now.

"Well, I think I've got you all beat," Kenny said triumphantly. "Yesterday, I found some really racy lingerie under the bed in one of my rooms."

"Really?" Rochelle exclaimed.

"Really. Black silk and lace; it's got to be really expensive."

I wonder what Nic would think of...I caught myself before I could finish the thought. Smiling to myself I bit into my sandwich. One cute guy and I was a total mess.

Chapter 3

"He's definitely the cutest guy here."

"Hands down. Even his eyes, he's definitely got Jeff beat."

"I know! That deep blue! And his smile is so dreamy. I swear I start drooling every time I see him."

I heard the girls going on as I walked up to the pool. They all had that glassy look that comes with dreaming about guys. "Who are you guys drooling over?" I asked, my t-shirt landed in an empty chair nearby, exposing my modest one piece swimming suit. Leaving my shorts on, I pushed my shirt aside and sat down.

"Nic," Tammy sighed. "I mean, he's just...perfect."

"And he's so nice, too!" Rochelle gushed.

"Yeah, I guess he is," I agreed, not wanting to them to know how smitten I already was with Nic. I knew exactly how sweet, and attractive, he was.

"Definitely has Jeff beat," Kenny said.

The girls all laughed, having been filled in on the catastrophe that was my date with Jeff.

We sat in silence for a few moments, soaking up the sun like it was the last day of summer. I let my mind wander from Nic, to school, to things back home. I didn't miss home as much as I thought I would and I felt a tinge of guilt creeping up. I should have been itching to get back to Esther, Scott, Todd and Sarah to help them navigate through the next few years without a mother but I wasn't. Instead, I was sitting in a pool chair at a mountain resort, thinking about the most good looking boy I'd ever laid eyes on.

"Vivian, look!" Kenny giggled, lowering herself onto the edge of my seat. "Tammy fell asleep. Can you believe it?" I looked over at Tammy's chair where, sure enough, she had drifted off to sleep.

Her sunhat had slipped down awkwardly over one eye and her mouth was hanging open.

"Poor girl," I said.

"Poor girl?" Rochelle countered. "If she's tired, that's what she gets for staying up all night flirting," she shook her head disapprovingly.

"Well, we can't all keep up with Kimi, now can we?" Kenny said. We watched as she laughed and flirted with a crowd of guys on the other side of the pool.

"Shameless," Rochelle laughed. "There must be something wrong with us. I think we're the only girls here who didn't come just to meet hot guys."

"Hey, I may be working but meeting hot guys is still on the agenda," Kenny joked.

"Did they run out of those at the YMCA?" Rochelle teased, leaning lazily against Kenny's arm.

"YMCA?" I asked. "Is that where you usually work?"

"Sort of, I volunteer," Kenny explained. "They always need help with classes, and I love hanging out with the kids. It's my home away from home, really."

"What kind of classes do you teach?" I pried, trying to picture Kenny teaching pottery or basket weaving.

"Basketball, volleyball, really any kind of sport," she laughed quietly. "The kids don't care if you're good at it, so it works out. I've met some really great people working there."

"She wants to be a social worker," Rochelle chimed in. "She's like Mother Teresa or something."

"Not even close to Mother Teresa," Kenny corrected. "But I do hate seeing what some of those kids go through. And I don't have any brothers or sisters, so they're kind of like my family."

"Wow," I said. "That's awesome. It sounds like you really found your place." I was in awe of Kenny's self-assuredness, and a feeling of inadequacy settled inside.

"What do you want to do, Rochelle?" I asked.

"I want to go to art school. Next semester I am hoping to go study abroad in Europe," she answered. It sounded like she had given this same answer several times before. "What about you, Vivian?"

"I'm not really sure where I'm going to end up yet," I answered. "I'm just trying to focus on my GEs right now. I've just been taking it one semester at a time. My mom was sick for a long time so money was really tight, and it got even worse after she passed away my senior year. I'm never really sure if we'll be able to find the money for my next semester, so I just do a couple classes and work as much as I can." I held my breath, realizing that I had probably said too much. I'd learned by now that talking about my mother, and about money, made people uncomfortable.

"Oh, Vivian, we had no idea," Kenny said. Her brow furrowed with concern and she put her arm around my shoulders. "Is that why you're working here this summer? To save for school?"

"Yeah. And it's been nice to get away from it all for a little while," I answered.

"I'm sure it has," Rochelle agreed. "So I guess now, we've got to help you figure out what you want to be when you grow up," she smiled mischievously. "How about a trophy wife?"

We all giggled.

"Find me a rich man and put me on the mantelpiece!" I said.

"Come on girls!" Alex yelled from the pool. "You can't just sit there all night! The water is perfect for some volleyball."

"You girls in?" Kenny asked, already taking off her shorts and t-shirt.

"For sure!" Rochelle answered poking Tammy. They got up and headed toward the pool. "You coming, Vivian?"

"Yep, I'm coming," I was tired from the day, but water volleyball did sound like fun. I could already imagine the cool water massaging my aching muscles. Pulling my hair back, I tied it up into a loose, messy bun, then wiggled out of my shorts and hurried to the pool. Sinking into the water, I saw Jeff walking through the gate into the pool area. I snatched a quick breath and slipped under the surface of the water and began to swim past the arms and legs floating around me. It seemed Jeff was finally getting the hint. I had heard rumors that he didn't appreciate me avoiding him for the last couple weeks. I was hoping that, with a little more time, the whole thing would blow over. I stood up in the chest deep water, breathing heavily for a moment.

"Watch out Vivian," Kenny yelled.

I looked up and felt a torrent of water pelt me in the face. I heard a deep, intoxicating laugh as I shook the water from my eyes. Sure enough, Nic had snuck in through the gate and cannonballed into the pool, catching everyone unaware. He laughed as some of the other guys tried to dunk his head under the water.

I stared at him. His wet hair hung down on his forehead and sent rivulets of water running down his face. He smiled constantly, as if his face didn't know any other expression. His voice was deep and strong as he joked and yelled with the other guys, his bare shoulders a gorgeous shade of summer.

"Come on, Viv!" Kenny called. "Let's play!"

A beach ball bounced lazily in front of me, drenching my face with cold water.

I did my best to snap out of it, but even as I chased the striped ball around the pool, my mind wasn't on the game. My eyes seemed to follow Nic wherever he went. His powerful swing always sent the ball soaring out of my reach, as well as emphasizing the sleek curves of his muscles. In a last minute effort to save the game, I set my jaw, determined to focus solely on the ball, but before he spiked it, Nic shot me a crooked grin and teasing wink. I stared for a moment too long, and the ball skirted right past my head, splashing into the water behind me.

"No!" Rochelle cried.

"Way to go, Nic!" Alex yelled.

"Take that, Kenny!" Tony jeered.

Kenny rolled her eyes and turned to the rest of the girls. "Whatever. It's just because they're taller than us," she reasoned. "If we'd been on sand, we would have wiped the floor with those guys."

"Ok, girls, let's show them what we got," Tammy cried.

The next thirty minutes were spent diving, hitting and chasing the ball. We gave the guys a run for their money but they still came out ahead. Tired and ready for a break we started to swim to the edge of the pool.

"Hey, girls!" Nic called. "Don't go yet. We just started. We'll mix it up, so it's not guys versus girls."

When no one replied, he smiled again, this time widening his eyes in a pleading look. "Come on!" he said. I melted, as it seemed he was talking just to me. After the other girls started to come back to the center of the pool, though, I realized that he had that effect on everybody.

Somehow, I ended up on his team. "You ready, Vivian?" he said, as he swam up to me.

"Yep," I answered, willing myself not to look directly into his eyes. That, I knew, was dangerous. I told myself to stop being so silly—he's just another guy. Really attractive, of course, but just another guy.

As the game started, I was already focusing more on the game. It was better having Nic on my team and not having him always in my line of sight. My limbs somehow seemed to regain their memory of the sport and I was able to hit the ball just as hard as I could on solid ground.

"Nice one, Vivian!" Nic cheered as I spiked the ball over the net.

"Thanks!" I laughed.

The ball skidded under the net to our side of the pool. "It's our serve; want me to set it for you?"

"Yeah, sure," I took my position in front of the net. Nic picked up the ball, tossed it up into the air, and slapped it in my direction with ease. With perfect timing, I vaulted up and brought my palm down on the ball. It sailed back toward the water on the other side of the net, clearing it by only a couple of inches. The others scrambled to reach it, belly flopping onto the water, but none of them could.

Tammy's serve sent the ball right to Kenny who returned it almost effortlessly. The ball seemed to fly smoothly back over the net. The bodies below scrambled to keep the ball airborne. The sound of laughter and the splashing of water skimmed around the pool for the next hour.

"Ha!" Nic hollered. "I told you we'd win!" He raised his arms to chest-level, and I assumed he was looking for a double high-five. But before I knew it, his thick arms were wrapped all the way around my shoulders, my cheek pressed against his smooth chest. Surprise caused me to take in a deeply tantalizing breath of chlorine and coconut. The laughter of the guys in the pool seemed to float away as Nic held me.

"Look out, Nic" I heard someone yell just before I was thrown off balance and was forced under the water by the weight above me. As Nic and I plunged into the water his grip around me tightened protectively around my waist. I held my breath, powerless to regain my balance. Water floated around me like a cool caress as I continued to sink deeper into the water, yet being held by Nic, I felt safe.

I felt the muscles of Nic's legs against mine as he kicked us to the surface. Water cascaded down his face, as he blinked and asked; "You okay there, Vivian?"

"I think so," I gasped.

"Good," he said matter-of-factly as his arms relaxed and fell to his side. I felt cold, despite the sun warming me, goosebumps arose on my shoulders where his skin had touched mine. I tried to keep myself afloat as I wiped the water out of my face.

"Watch out," Tony yelled.

I glanced over in time to see Kenny jump up out of the water to get the ball, and land with a splash, pushing me under with her.

I sputtered to the surface.

"I think I am done for a while," I said as I tried to catch my breath.

"Sorry about that," Kenny said.

"Let's go sit in the sun for a bit," Nic said.

I nodded and swam to the edge of the pool, Nic at my side. A slight breeze tickled my skin as I pulled myself out of the water. Rubbing my arms briskly I looked around for a towel. Spying the stack on a nearby table I hurried over and snatched two, handing one to Nic. I couldn't help but admire his long muscular legs and his powerfully built, tanned chest.

Looking away I said, "Want to sit over there?" pointing to two lounge chairs.

"So where are you from?" he asked after we had dried off and were stretched out bathing in the sun.

"Northern Utah, just a small town there," I answered.

"How did you end up here then?" he asked.

"I saw a job posting on the bulletin board at my community college. I needed a job, and I wanted to leave home for a while," I realized that left room for more questions, so I cleared my throat and changed the subject before he could ask any of them. "What about you? How'd you end up here?"

"Hey Nic!" A slim girl wearing a blue bikini said as she walked by. I thought I recognized her as one of the waitresses from the café. I blushed and looked down at my towel, grateful that it was covering my legs. I told myself that I should have worn shorts over my bathing suit.

But instead of talking to her, Nic just nodded and gave her a slight smile. I couldn't believe it when, almost immediately, he turned his gaze back to me.

"I'm from Colorado," he answered, as if they'd never been interrupted. "My friend, Jackie McKinnon, worked here one summer after high school. She told me about it, and when I graduated a year later I decided to come too."

"I didn't know you and Jackie were from the same town," I said.

"Yeah, our families are good friends," he smiled. "Anyway, I've been here for three summers now. It's laid back and the scenery up here is incredible! I've got a new camera that I'm looking forward to trying out.

"You're a photographer?" I asked.

"Well, it's more of a hobby right now, but yeah."

"I've always loved photography," I explained. "All I have is small Kodak pocket camera my dad gave me years ago. But who knows, maybe by the end of the summer I'll have a little extra money to spend on one," I said with a smile.

"Well, in the meantime," Nic began, "I have an extra one. And there are a lot of great places around that I haven't been to yet," he smiled sideways at me. "You could come with me sometime."

I rolled over until I was facing Nic, my hand shading my eyes. "Really? I said, "that sounds great."

"What about you?" Nic asked. "What do you like to do?"

"Well," I said, "I like music; I play the piano a little and the guitar."

"Do you have your guitar here?" Nic asked.

I nodded.

"You'll have to play for me sometime."

"Maybe," I said smiling a little as I rolled onto my back.

I closed my eyes and lay there basking in the warmth of the sun and our conversation.

Chapter 4

"Here are your room assignments for today," Sylvia said as she passed the stack of papers around the room.

Flipping through the pile I found mine and pulled it out.

"All but one room is a 'check-out," I groaned.

"At least you have one easy room, I don't have any," moaned Rochelle.

"Good luck," I said as I found my cart and headed out the door.

A long forgotten memory moved to the front of my mind as I pulled my loaded cart down the long hall toward my first room of the day.

I was in a red wagon, racing down the sidewalk, the steep incline pulling me faster and faster, the metal handle jerking in my small, sweaty fists. Feeling it slip from my grasp, I screamed as the wagon flipped and I skidded across the sidewalk. I rolled across the thinning grass to a stop, the wagon dropped in a cloud of dust to land beside my shaking form.

The bathroom counter felt cold beneath my short legs in contrast to the burning on my knees. Bubbles from the hydrogen peroxide fizzled as my dad cleaned the rocks and dirt out. I couldn't stop the sobs every time he touched me. More tears fell with every painful pinch of the tweezers in my dad's hand. The soft washcloth that had gently wiped away my tears now tore at the flesh of my knees as he scrubbed away the dirt.

I nearly toppled over as my cart bumped me from behind. I had stopped and was rubbing my knee. Where had that come from? Making a mental note to write it down that evening I pulled the cart to my first room and got to work.

"Man what a day," Rochelle said as she flopped on her bed, one leg dangling off.

"I didn't think I would ever get finished," I responded as I kicked off my shoes and commenced rubbing my feet. "At least I have the swan thing down."

"What do you want to do tonight?"

"How about teaching me how to paint?" I said looking over at her.

I watched as she lifted her head off the bed and looked at me skeptically.

"I'm serious; the water colors you had spread out on your bed the other day were beautiful. I've never done anything but paint by number. That seems a bit too childish now, don't you think?"

"Ok, I guess I could teach you some basics."

"Let's go get something to eat first, I'm famished."

Changing into shorts and t-shirts we slipped on our flip flops and ambled down the hall.

"Hey, wait up," Rochelle called to Kimi and Tammy. We exited the building and walked down the gravel road.

"I'm beat," Kimi said. "After dinner I just want to sprawl out on a towel by the pool and take a nap."

"I'm right there with you," Tammy said.

I looked over at Rochelle who shook her head slightly; I smiled keeping the painting lesson to ourselves.

It didn't take long to pick up some dinner and find Kenny in the almost deserted cafeteria. Sinking into one of the vacant seats I took a bite of my hamburger.

"Hey girls," Kyle said, approaching us with an empty plate in his hands. "We're going to get a fire going outside. You should come hang with us."

"I don't know, Kyle," Kenny answered. "We're all pretty beat."

"Come on, it'll be fun. We're just gonna sit around the fire and chill"

"Sounds good."

"I'm in."

"Okay," she answered. "We've just got to clear up and we'll meet you out there." Kyle gave us a nod and headed for the door.

I leaned over to Rochelle and whispered," You still get to teach me how to paint."

She smiled as we stood.

"It'll be fun," Rochelle said. "Campfires always are. Kyle may even bring his ocarina."

"What's that?"

"Wait and see, I think you'll love it."

By the time everyone had gathered by the big rock fire pit, it was just getting dark. Kyle and Alex fiddled around with kindling and logs, trying to get the fire going. Finally, despite the breeze, the scent of a fire joined the smells of fresh grass and pine. To my dismay, I noticed Jeff sitting a few chairs away from me in the circle. I looked away, crossed my legs up on the chair and pulled them close to me.

A bag of marshmallows and some long sticks lay on a bench on the other side of the fire.

"You want one?" Rochelle asked as she stood up.

"No, you go ahead," I said. "I'm not really in the mood."

"Your loss," she said grinning as she walked away.

The fire enveloped me in its warmth. Conversation flowed as the rhythmic movement of the flames drew me in. I stared, mesmerized by their exotic and mysterious dance. The crackling of burning wood and the quiet call of the crickets bathed me with a comforting sense of peace and security. Stars shimmered and sparkled in the ever darkening sky.

The scraping of a chair ripped me away from space that held me and I turned to see Jeff sit down next to me.

"I'm sorry about the other night," he said glancing over at me. "I didn't mean to make you wait. I was late getting off work." He turned away and looked at the ground.

"Don't worry about it," I said.

He seemed a little different tonight. I thought he would be upset because I had been avoiding him. But he didn't seem mad, just the opposite. Maybe our date was just a fluke and he really wasn't that bad.

"So, have you had a chance to go into town yet?" he asked looking back to me.

I shook my head.

"I could take you sometime?" he asked. "To make up for being late."

"Maybe," I said, taken a little off guard by the question.

I was a little surprised that he was asking me out again. Should I give him another chance?

"There's some great stores we could check out," he said. "I know how girls love to shop."

"All right," I said.

"I'll let you know when I have a day off," he said as he got up to leave.

Rochelle came scurrying around the other side of the fire. I had no idea why she was in such a rush.

She flopped into the recently vacated chair and leaned over excitedly and whispered, "Shut your eyes."

"What? Why?"

"Just close your eyes."

I laid my head back on the chair and closed my eyes. Out of the darkness arose a sound so soft and soothing, I didn't dare move for fear it would end. The melody seemed to just float on a gentle breeze. The voices around me faded and eventually disappeared as I was caught up in the serene beauty of the music. The notes seemed to hang, suspended on the stars, and then faded away across the sky.

Chapter 5

I heard the creaking of saddles and felt the strength of the horse beneath me. The narrow trail was edged by tall aspens, the leaves fluttered as the branches moved in the wind. I looked around at the beautiful scenery and noticed another rider ahead of me. I urged my horse forward. The closer I got I could tell that the man rode with a natural confidence. He reminded me of Nic.

I woke up slowly remembering the man on the horse. Smiling to myself I thought that's one dream I would like to see happen. Stretching, I looked over at my clock. Only 8:32. I snuggled back down in the warmth of the blankets relishing in the lazy morning. Looking out the window across the room I admired the grandeur of the mountains.

A quiet tap at the door pulled my thoughts back into the room. Rochelle groaned and turned over, pulling her covers over her head. I slipped out from under the comforter and tiptoed over to the door. It was a girl from the across the hall.

"You have a phone call, Vivian," she said quietly. It occurred to me that Rochelle probably wasn't the only girl still asleep, although I couldn't imagine sleeping past nine.

"Okay, thanks. I'm coming," I took one more look at Rochelle, still just a lump under the covers, and followed the other girl down the hall.

"Cute PJs," the girl said, smiling.

"Oh, thanks," I replied, glancing down at my pink and gray plaid pajama pants and gray tank top. At the end of the hall, next to the bathrooms, the community phone sat on the wall above a rickety little table. I sat down on an old black plastic chair and picked up the receiver.

"Hello?" I said, twisting the phone cord between my fingers. I wracked my brain, but I couldn't think of anyone who would be calling me here and especially that early in the morning.

"Hey Vivian," was the suave reply.

"Nic?" I said incredulously. I found myself patting down my mussed hair with my free hand.

"Good morning," he said cheerfully. He had managed to throw me off guard again, and he knew it. From his voice, I could tell that he was even a little bit proud of it.

"Good morning," I said. I hadn't gotten any calls before, so I didn't realize how public the phone area was. As girls came in and out of the bathroom, I found myself wishing for a little bit of privacy. "What's up?"

"Well, it's a beautiful day out and the light is perfect for taking pictures. Do you want to go do a shoot with me?"

"Yeah, that sounds great. Can you give me...20 minutes?"

"Of course; meet me in the cafeteria when you're ready, okay?"

"Yeah. I'll be there. Where are we going?" I asked.

"You'll find out," Nic said mischievously. "But I would recommend you wear some good hiking shoes."

I smiled. "Okay. I'll see you in a bit." The phone clicked in my ear as Nic hung up, but it was a few seconds before I could put the receiver down. I walked back down the hallway to my room, a smile on my flushed face. I was going on a date with Nic. I quickened my pace, hoping I could find something decent to wear.

Fifteen minutes later, I emerged from the cabin clad in a fitted hot pink t-shirt, one that my sister Esther had always said looked great on me, and brown shorts. Though I knew my sandals were more stylish, I chose to wear my not so fashionable hiking boots. The last thing I wanted was to end up with blisters and splinters while I was out with Nic. I pulled my thick hair into a braid that hung over my shoulder.

I was halfway to the dining room when I heard a familiar voice. "Hey Viv!" Jeff called. "Wait up!" He came jogging up to me with an impish grin on his face. I forced a smile back at him, fighting the urge to turn and walk away.

"I was thinking that on your next day off we could go into town? Walk around a bit, see some sites?" he proposed. He looked at me expectantly.

"I don't know, Jeff," I began.

"There's this concert in the park we could go to."

"Who's playing?" I said trying to be polite.

"I don't know but I bet they're good," he said.

I was quickly getting bored with this conversation. I looked towards the cafeteria where Nic was waiting.

"So..." he urged. "Next week?" He smiled broadly.

"Yeah, ok." I replied at last. What harm could there be in giving him a second chance?

"I've got plans with Kenny and some other girls in the morning, but I should be free by one. We could hang out then."

"Great, I'll plan on it. We could meet at the park in the center of town," Jeff winked, and ran off. Nic was much better at winking.

I smiled when I saw Nic waving to me from the breakfast table.

"Hey beautiful!" he said, walking towards me. "You ready to have some fun?"

"Definitely."

"Good. Come on." He swung a pack over his shoulder took my hand and led me out to the parking lot. I stared in utter amazement at our linked hands as we walked, wondering why he had taken mine. I wondered if he always did this, or if it was possible that he only did this with me. I tried to understand, but with Nic there was no telling. I couldn't even tell if it was my palm or his that had started to sweat, but either way I prayed he didn't notice. Even so, I didn't want him to let go.

"Nicholas Ryan. Where are you headed off to so early?" a voice called after us.

Nic turned, still grasping my hand. "My beautiful girl!" he answered cheerfully. Jackie had caught up to them and had taken her place next to me. "We're gonna go take some pictures."

"Oh, that sounds wonderful!" Jackie gushed. "I, on the other hand am off to work." She rolled her eyes and pursed her lips in exaggerated annoyance. "But we should do something later."

"For sure. See you!" Nic said.

"See you! Bye Vivian," Jackie smiled.

"Bye Jackie," I replied. He'd called her beautiful too, and I was beginning to wonder if he would have taken her instead, if it hadn't been for her breakfast shift. The magic of the morning was slowly fading, and I felt the cold fingers of jealousy creeping in. But when Nic started to walk and pulled me along with the gentle pressure of his hand, I buried that feeling. What mattered was that I was going to spend the next few hours with Nic. It would be just the two of us and nothing was going to ruin it.

"So, there's this amazing lake we could hike to," Nic began. "The hike is kind of long, but the view is unbelievable. You down?" he asked

"Sure," I agreed. How could I say no?

"So, the dining room didn't really have anything, but I do know this great little place we could stop and get something to take with us. And there are some great views on the way."

"Then let's go," I smiled up at him.

We came to a stop next to a new-looking silver jeep. Nic pulled open the door. I hopped in and fastened my seatbelt, all the while trying to wipe the cheesy grin off my face. Nic climbed in and started up the jeep. Gravel flipped as we headed out of the parking lot.

"So tell me about yourself," Nic said as he pulled onto the highway.

"Well, what do you want to know?"

Chapter 6

"Wow. How did you find this place? It's so beautiful," I asked, as I lifted my eyes to the rampant wildflowers on the green mountainside. I was glad the dusty trail was wide enough so that we could walk beside each other. Nic had said the lake was just a few miles down the trail when he pulled the jeep into the turnout by the trailhead.

"I know. Jackie brought me here last summer and it's been my favorite place ever since. Just to come to think and be alone, you know?" I smiled at him, thinking how at home he looked up here in the hills.

"Yeah," I agreed quietly. "This is like heaven, I haven't had much alone time lately."

"Really?" Nic asked, raising an eyebrow. "Why not?"

I kicked the dirt, feeling the melancholy come slithering back. "Well, "I said, "my mom died a while back, so I've been trying to help my dad out, you know, with my siblings and stuff. And I've been going to school and working part-time too so I just haven't had a whole lot of free time." I braced myself for the pity and the reassurances that usually followed this explanation, but it never came.

"I bet you haven't," Nic smiled even wider. "All the more reason for us to take advantage of such a fantastic day." I could feel the strength in his warm calloused hand as he took hold of mine. "Come on, there's a nice little path down this way." I didn't resist as he led me down the trail through the trees. The leafy canopy over our heads filled the air with a green glow and the warm pungent smell of pine needles under our feet.

We walked in silence for about half an hour before the trees began to spread out. Warm sunlight streamed in through the ever widening spaces as Nic pulled me off the trail into a wide clearing. Velvety green grass carpeted the rolling meadow dotted with brightly colored wildflowers of reds and yellows. A few fallen logs were lazily strewn about. To me, it looked like a scene from a fairytale; like any moment a castle would appear on top of the hill.

"How about here for breakfast?" Nic asked, gesturing to the clearing.

"Sounds great," I said.

"Not bad, huh?" Nic ushered me over to one of the fallen logs. "Here, sit down. I'll get everything ready." I did as he said, realizing now that my legs were getting tired and stiff. The moss on the log made for a comfortable cushion and, as Nic rummaged around in his backpack, I let myself relax. I planted my palms on the log and tilted my face up to the cloudless blue sky, taking in the warm sun with my eyes closed.

"Don't move," Nic commanded. His voice startled me and I flinched and opened my eyes but I didn't move.

"What's wrong?" I asked. "Is there a snake?" I instinctively began to pull my feet up off the ground.

"No, just don't move. The light is perfect." His voice was deadly serious, but I realized that he had gotten out his camera and had it focused on me.

"What are you—" I exclaimed, turning red.

"Beautiful!" Nic interrupted. "What a shot."

I looked at him with wide eyes.

"What?" he said innocently. "Can't a photographer take a picture of a beautiful girl?"

As much as I tried to hold it in, I let out a little chuckle, half embarrassed, half flattered. I lifted one hand to my face, brushing the same old section of hair behind my ear. As I did, I heard the camera click again.

"I thought we were supposed to be taking pictures of the lake," I said.

"Oh, just a few more; we have plenty of film." He looked up from behind the camera, making a sad face. "Please?" he begged.

I laughed and he snapped another picture. "Gorgeous!" he called, walking around with the camera. I kept laughing, and he kept taking pictures. I felt giddy and totally disbelieving that this incredible guy would be so interested in me, calling me beautiful and gorgeous. It was strange but wonderful

"I think I got it," Nic said finally, lowering his camera. "Now, I believe it's time I got you some breakfast. I can hear your stomach rumbling from here." He slung the backpack off his shoulders and sat down next to me. He pulled out the brown paper sacks full of the pastries we had bought on the way. "Okay, do you want the chocolate muffin, chocolate croissant, or the blueberry muffin?" he eyed me expectantly.

"I think I will try the chocolate muffin," I said.

Nic took the muffin out of the bag but instead of handing it to me he pulled of a portion and lifted it to my mouth. A little surprised, I took a bite and felt the moist, chocolate melt across my tongue. I clasped my hands together, hoping he couldn't see them shaking. I felt out of place; not pretty enough or sophisticated enough for this to be happening to me.

"So, what do you think?"

I chewed slowly, savoring the rich chocolaty flavor. "It's really, really good." I answered finally.

"I love chocolate muffins." I said as I reached out to take the muffin from his outstretched hand.

"Just wait til you try the croissant," he said.

With the pastries finished, Nic crinkled up the paper bag and put it in his backpack and pulled out his extra camera. "Here," he said, holding it in front of me, "let me show you how it works."

He scooted a little closer until his thigh brushed up against mine. I relished the closeness of the moment. I paid more attention to the pressure of his leg than his breakdown of the camera. I heard his voice, but somehow it seemed more like music than instructions as he explained how to focus the lens and zoom in and out on a subject. He was perfect, absolutely perfect.

"Got it?" Nic asked suddenly. I felt certain that he knew what I was thinking.

"Yeah, I think so," I replied. "But are you sure you have enough film? I don't want to waste it."

"Don't worry about it. I brought plenty. And I have more back in my room, too." He offered me the camera, and as I took it my fingers brushed over his strong, calloused ones.

I lifted the camera nervously from his hand and stood up. I put the cold plastic to my eye and looked through the lens, adjusting it to clear the blurriness. As I fiddled with the lens, Nic's arm reached around to follow the curve of mine. His muscles were taut as he put his hand undermine to help me steady the camera.

"Thanks," I said as the red flowers I had been focusing on blurred.

I don't know if it was because I was using his camera and that made him nervous but Nic didn't stray far from my side for the next hour. It's like he kept making up excuses to help me focus the camera or give me tips about lighting. I wonder if he took any pictures during that time. It was very distracting in a very appealing way.

The lake, when we finally reached it, was the color of the early morning sky. Surrounding it on three sides were tall, tree covered mountains. Wild flowers grew in an array of color across the lower slopes and falling down to the water's edge. So many images I wanted to capture, I didn't know where to begin.

The camera seemed at home in my hands and, despite not having paid attention to Nic's instructions, handling came instinctively. I managed to capture a few chipmunks as they scurried up a tree trunk, and a moose that was hiding behind the trees foraging around in the undergrowth. But for all the beauty of the mountains and lake, my 35mm camera kept going back to Nic. He was gorgeous, that much was certain, but there was something else beneath the surface that kept me drawn in. I captured on film, pieces of perfection that I could keep with me even if I never saw him again after the summer ended.

It was late afternoon when we made it back to the jeep. Nic kept sending me sideways glances and crooked grins and nudging my shoulder as he joked. It was perfect in an unfamiliar sort of way, and then we were back at the resort. My stomach sunk as we walked from the parking lot, getting closer and closer to my cabin. His arm was draped loosely around my shoulder, and I thought it must be the only thing keeping my feet planted on the ground.

By the time we reached the cabin door I wondered. What should I say? Should I hug him? Just wave and say thanks? But before I could do anything, Nic tightened his grip on my shoulders and pulled me into his chest. I took a deep breath in, smelling the scent of pine trees that lingered around him. Slowly, I relaxed and let my own arms slide around his back, returning the hug.

"Thanks for coming with me," Nic said quietly as he stepped back. "It was a really great day."

"It was wonderful. Thank—" Nic leaned in as I spoke and placed his lips gently on my face, dangerously close to mine. His breath tickled the corner of my lips and raised goose bumps all over my body.

Our eyes met for a second. HIs soft, warm and liquid blue, "I'll see you later, Vivian."

"Yeah," I breathed. My arms fell to my side as he walked away. I stood still until he was out of sight, unsure that my legs would support me if I moved.

"Wow!" I giggled as I leaned back against the wall.

"Is that you Viv?" I heard Rochelle call from inside the room.

"Yes," I said as I opened the door and went inside.

"Looks like someone had a good day," Rochelle said.

"It was way beyond a good day," I said grinning.

"Oh my gosh, these thighs!" Tammy whined. "I mean, look at my thighs," she commanded, lifting her leg up off the pool chair. "They're huge!"

"Oh please!" Rochelle countered. "They're perfect. Nothing compared to these love handles."

I wrapped my arms around my stomach to hide my not-too-flat stomach. It didn't matter what the scale said, I had seen myself in a bikini, and wasn't ready to wear one out in public—at least not until I'd fixed the flaws.

"Well, I think you're all gorgeous," Kenny complimented. "You put those bikini-wearing pool-tarts to shame!" She stood up, doing her best imitation of the aspiring models that patrolled the pool calling themselves "life-guards."

"Good one, Kenny," Kimi giggled.

"We may be gorgeous," I said, "but I could definitely use some exercise. I wouldn't mind dropping a few pounds."

"What few pounds?" Tammy argued. "Honey, you've got the least pounds out of all of us."

"Just a few. Like ten or so," I cringed, almost wishing I hadn't said anything. That's what people always said when I mentioned the weight I wanted to lose. "Besides, even if I'm skinny, I could always be in better shape. On my hike today I was pretty out of breath and it was an easy hike."

"I think you're right," Kenny agreed, putting me at ease somewhat. "Maybe we could all do something together, like go running or something,"

"Um, running? No way," Rochelle declared. "I have a better idea. I help out with a yoga class a few times a week; you guys could come try it out."

"Yoga?" Tammy said skeptically. "I don't know..."

"Oh, come on. It'll be fun," Rochelle assured them.

"Now about that hike," Kenny said turning to me, beaming.

Chapter 7

"Earth to Vivian. You in there?" Tammy prodded, waving her hand back and forth in front of my eyes.

I shook my head, trying to snap myself back into reality. "Yeah, yeah I'm here," I answered. "Sorry, I just zoned out for a minute." I smiled and nodded as the other girls planned out the next day's big shopping trip in town. I was excited about the outing, but my mind kept wandering until it seemed that I was somewhere else. Another place, another time.

I'd been deep in a forest, only able to make out the silhouettes of several other people in the dim green light. I was agitated and unsure. Fear careened to the surface. The arrow that had been pressing against my throat began to fall. Capturing it, I took a step back. My breath ragged as I stood there shaking. I can do this I said as if trying to talk myself into believing that I really could. Closing my eyes and breathing deeply I worked to calm my frantic heart. Sounds of support seeped through the turbulence in my mind. Opening my eyes I stepped before the tree, placing the feathered end against the solid trunk I set the cold, metal point of the arrow against my throat and began to lean forward. The arrow bent at the pressure. My eyes remained focused on the curve of the wooden shaft. With one last fragment of courage I pressed forward. CRACK!

I shook my head again, rubbing my fingers against my throat.

"What's up Vivian?" Kenny asked. "You keep spacing out. Are you sure you're okay?"

"Yea," I said, straightening up. "I'm sorry. I was just thinking of..."

"Nic, I bet," Tammy said.

"I saw him in the restaurant a few times this week. It looked like he was pretty busy," Kimi said.

"I've got an idea," Rochelle said. "Why don't we start our day off early and treat ourselves to dinner?"

"Maybe Nic will be our waiter," Kimi smirked.

"I'm definitely not wearing these cutoffs," I remarked, sliding off the bed.

"Wait for me," called Rochelle. "I'm going to change too; you never know how many cute waiters will be working tonight."

I could hear Tammy and Kimi's laughter follow us as we hightailed it to our room.

The restaurant was almost deserted, only a few couples dotted the room. Chamber music drifted quietly as we relaxed at our table tucked under a window overlooking the patio.

"Evening ladies," Nic's voice was deep and smooth.

I looked up to see him flash a dazzling smile in my direction. His crisp, white shirt hugged his broad chest. The short black apron he wore hung snug and low on his hips

"What brings you here tonight?"

"Well, Vivian has been...Ow," Kimi said. "Who kicked me?"

"We just decided to do a little something out of the ordinary tonight," I said getting Nic's attention.

"I guess this is out of the ordinary since it's the first time I've seen you in here all summer," he remarked.

After placing our orders Nic strode back to the kitchen. Mine weren't the only eyes following him that night.

Chicago blared out of the boom box as we danced around the bedroom, collapsing in a fit of laughter as the last notes of Prima Donna faded.

"What are you guys shopping for tomorrow?" Tammy asked as we lay there trying to recover from our crazy dance moment. "I'm hoping to find a new swimsuit and a dress.

"Oh, me too!" Rochelle exclaimed.

I, too, wanted a new swimsuit. Before I knew it, I found myself wondering what Nic would like on me. I couldn't get him out of my mind. Especially after the attention he showed me tonight. Every thought led to him eventually. That day at the lake had been magical. There had been moments when I'd thought he must like me, but a wink at Kenny or a "hello beautiful" to Jackie, and I started second guessing everything.

"Oh shoot!" my train of thought finally wandering from Nic and the dream.

"What's wrong?" Kenny asked.

"I forgot. I told Jeff that I would meet him in town after shopping tomorrow. I really don't want to, but I think it's too late to get out of it," I rolled over, staring at the ceiling, dreading the impending date.

"I know something that will take your mind off of it," Jackie said mischievously.

"Do tell," Kimi said.

"Well, here at the resort, we ladies have a tradition. No boys allowed." She gave a crooked grin and continued, milking our curiosity. "Up the river about 10 minutes, there are some hot springs. Every year, at least once, we wait until dark and sneak up there to go skinny dipping."

Rochelle, Tammy, and I gasped. Kimi hid her face with her hands and shrieked.

"So what do you say, girls? Late night swim tonight?" Jackie's piercing blue eyes were looking straight at me.

"Uhhh... Su—," I began sitting up.

"I want to go," Kenny declared. "And Vivian will come too." She linked her arm through mine, ignoring the stunned look that had crept onto my face.

"You bet I'm coming," Tammy smiled.

"Me to," giggled Kimi.

"Great," Jackie said. "I've got to take off but I will meet you back here in an hour." She was smiling, but I couldn't help but hear a hint of something mischievous in her voice.

Nervous chatter flew through the room after Jackie left.

"Did you do this last year?" I asked.

"I did," Tammy said. "It was a blast."

"I was gone that night," Rochelle said. "Kind of wish I was gone tonight," she whispered.

"Are you really going?" Rochelle asked later as we rummaged through our dressers, pulling out our swimsuits.

"I guess so," I answered. "Kenny didn't really give me much choice. How about you?"

"Oh, I'll go. But don't expect me to take off my suit."

"Yeah..." I mused. "I don't know about that."

Once our swimsuits were on, we slipped into our flip flops and walked back to Kenny's room with our towels under our arms. The other girls were waiting outside the door, whispering excitedly.

"All right," Jackie declared. "Let's hit it."

Outside, the full moon illuminated the trail all the way from the cabin to the river. The trees cast shadows on the graveled path and despite the warm air, my arms and shoulders were prickling with goose bumps. I clamped my fingers around my towel, anxiously anticipating what we were about to do. I went back and forth, unable to decide if I would or not. On a normal day I felt out of place in my swimsuit, but right now it seemed pretty comfortable, much more comfortable than stripping down to my skin and jumping into the water with a bunch of other girls.

"Have you ever been caught?" Tammy asked as we neared the springs.

"No," Jackie answered proudly. "But we've had a few close calls. Most of the supervisors know, because they've done it, but they just keep it quiet. Only one or two are actually strict enough to try to stop us, if they knew," she laughed. "Last year a friend and I went just an hour too early and we had to throw our towels on and hide in the trees for an hour to escape this couple that showed up."

We followed the river around a bend to a secluded ox-bow section. Trees huddled together, shielding the hot springs. It was almost comforting.

Jackie approached a wide, flat rock that was half-submerged in the steamy water. "Put your stuff here," she instructed. "It won't get wet, and it's easier than looking around in the dark for your clothes.

I looked to see what Jackie was talking about, but what I saw was her blue bikini slide off and hit the ground. Bending over, she grabbed them and tossed them haphazardly onto the rock; then jumped into the hot water.

I was sure that if it hadn't been dark the other girls would have seen the jealousy blatant across my face as I watched her. With a skinny body like that, of course she had no qualms about being naked in front of people.

"Hey let's go," Kenny whispered to me. "We can't let Jackie have all the fun."

"You know what," I declared. "You're right."

Kenny and I began to undress. Who cared if Jackie had a perfect body, and I didn't? I'd spent enough of my life hiding, and this could have been a once-in-a-lifetime chance to be reckless and crazy and completely at ease with myself. I tore off my swimsuit and jumped into the water. I heard the girls cheering as my head went under. It was warmer than I had expected, sending little pinpricks up and down my body. But I felt free. Coming up out of the water, I took a gulp of air and smiled at Kenny.

She was taking her time getting in the water, stepping in carefully, doing her best to cover her chest with her arms. Her discomfort was obvious, which was strange for me to see. Kenny always seemed so sure of herself, a natural leader. I started to realize for the first time this summer that maybe I wasn't the only one who felt a little out of place in her own body.

Kimi was next, giggling uncontrollably as she stripped off her suit. "Oh my gosh, this is crazy!" she shouted. But she strutted around on the bank for a few seconds before jumping in. I laughed, admiring her ability to make even the most awkward situations fun.

Tammy sidled into the water with her suit still on. Neck deep, she slipped the straps off her shoulders and removed her bathing suit. Keeping it clutched to her chest reluctant to let it go.

I smiled and rolled over onto my back, floating in the water and looking up at the moon. I knew my not-quite-flat stomach was poking just above the water, but I didn't care.

"This is nuts," Rochelle whispered, moving over by me. "Absolutely nuts."

"Did you leave your suit on?" I asked, lowering my legs to stand in the water.

She looked down at the water with a tiny crooked smile.

"No!" Even in the dim light I could see her cheeks flare up.

"Good for you!" I said.

"Isn't this great?" Jackie sighed. "Just us girls. No boys to bother us. We don't even have to worry about whether or not our hair looks good, let alone the fact that we're all naked." Kimi's signature giggle rang out again.

"Shh!" Tammy ordered, trying not to laugh herself. "Really Kimi, I don't think you could be any louder if you tried."

"Sorry," Kimi snorted, covering her mouth with her hands. "I was just thinking, what would those guys do if they saw us like this?" Kenny sent a big splash at her.

"Hopefully they'd be perfect gentlemen and pretend they hadn't seen anything," Kenny said.

"Hopefully?" Kimi said incredulously. "You and I have very different hopes, honey. I hope they'd remember, and at the very least I'd get a date."

I couldn't help but laugh. Half of me agreed with Kenny, but the other half wasn't totally convinced that Kimi was in the wrong.

"Well, let's just hope they don't show up here," Tammy said, clutching her swimsuit even tighter. "I think I would die if Alex saw me like this."

"I knew it!" Rochelle cried, splashing Tammy right in the face. "I knew you had a thing for Alex!"

"And I know you have a thing for Kyle," Tammy countered. "But I think he's a bit short for you."

"Who cares how tall he is?" Rochelle answered. "Have you seen those muscles? His six pack is unreal."

They went back and forth, arguing the virtues of Alex and Kyle. Soon Kenny joined in talking about Tony, too, but I didn't have anything to add. Once I saw Nic, those other guys all but ceased to exist, six packs and all.

I didn't realize how long we'd been in the water until my fingers began to prune. I knew it must be late, and I had work in the morning, but I didn't want to go. Between the warm fresh water and the gentle, almost-cool breeze, the temperature was perfect. Once I got out the spell would be broken and I would be painfully aware of my body again.

"Thanks for making me come," I told Jackie. "It was amazing, really."

"It's too bad the summer is almost over. I would love to do this again," Kenny added.

"Me too," Jackie sighed. "You should all come back next summer. It wouldn't be the same without you guys."

I wished that I could plan that far ahead, but I knew that as soon as I got home I would go back to living my life a day at a time, worrying about money and school and my family.

"Quiet!" Tammy shrieked. "Do you hear that?"

"Someone's coming!" Jackie confirmed. "Get out, hurry!" We all leaped out of the water and grabbed our things off the rock. I followed the other girls into the trees and dried off as best we could. As I struggled to pull my swimsuit on over my sticky damp skin, I heard several voices coming down the path. Kimi's eyes widened when she realized who it was; Alex, Kyle, Tony, and Nic. Kenny clamped her hand over Kimi's mouth before she could make a sound and give us away.

There was just enough light from the moon that we could see the guys as they got closer. Much more at ease than we had been, they pulled off their clothes and tossed them carelessly on the rock before taking turns doing cannonballs into the water. I couldn't take my eyes off Nic as he undressed. In the moonlight I could see the skin on his back was smooth and tight over well-defined muscles. I had never seen such definition on a guy's backside before. Not that I had seen a guy's backside before. But a girl can imagine, can't she? His was perfect.

While Tammy and Rochelle stifled laughter, Jackie whispered; "Let's steal their clothes." Kimi nodded excitedly. Kenny gave a thumbs up. Before I could process what we were about to do, we had crept forward from the tree line, keeping low to the ground. This was crazy! I couldn't help but smile.

We crouched down behind some bushes, waiting for Jackie's signal. She held up three fingers and mouthed, "Three, two, one!"

"Hi boys," she said as we all stood up.

I watched as Nic and the others plunged deeper into the water.

"A little careless, don't you think? Leaving your clothes just lyin' around," Jackie taunted. "Anyone could just pick them up and walk away," she said as she walked over to the rock and picked up a pair of shorts, swinging it between her slender fingers.

"Hey, put that down, those are mine," Alex yelled.

"Did you want to get out and make me?" she said laughing.

Alex scowled.

"Come on girls, grab the clothes!"

With that we rushed the rock, taking what we could before the guys reached us in their frantic race to get their clothes. The other girls tore off down the path, their arms full. I stayed just long enough to blow a kiss and see the look on Nic's face before running after them. Maybe it was just my imagination, but I could have sworn there was just a little bit of admiration in his eyes.

Chapter 8

The aroma of bacon hit me like a wave sliding on the shore, as I walked up to the counter. Stacks of golden brown pancakes filled the serving tray as well as piles of bright yellow scrambled eggs. A large mountain of crispy bacon lay ready for the taking.

"What would you like this morning?" Jessie asked. "The oatmeal pancakes just came off the grill and are absolutely delicious."

"That sounds really good. How about some eggs and one of those bowls of fruit to go with it?" I said as I eyed the assortment of fruit in the small, glass bowls sunk deep in crushed ice.

"Great choice," said Jessie.

"Why not just have the Captain Crunch, like me," said Jeff.

I turned towards the sound. He was standing next to me with a large bowl of dried, yellow, tasteless cereal and a glass of milk on his tray.

I shrugged. "No thanks".

"We're still on for town today. I'll see you in the park at 1:00," he said,

"Ya, ok I'll see you then," I said, turning back to the food.

"I hope you enjoy your breakfast," Jessie said as I reached out to get a glass of chocolate milk. I glanced up at her and saw a look of curiosity cross her usually serene face.

I gave her a halfhearted smile and turned to find a seat.

Weaving through the crowded cafeteria I saw Kenny waving frantically from the corner. I absently meandered over to her table and sat down with a sigh.

"What's up?" asked Kenny, looking at me as I just sat there staring at my plate of pancakes.

"Thinking about Jeff, are you?" she said half laughing.

My eyes flew up to meet Kenny's.

"No," I hissed.

"Nice to see you back; where have you been? You seemed miles away."

My mind jumped back to the dream from the night before. I'd had a lot of dreams in my life but this one was just downright naughty.

"Sorry, I had a dream last night when we got back from the river and I can't figure it out.

"What happened?" Kenny asked.

"Well, I was up at a really nice resort. There were about 8-10 people there, both guys and girls. We were all hanging out around this amazing pool. It had waterfalls and hot tubs. The landscape was astonishing. Flowers of every color and immense trees shading paths that took you to other more secluded pools. It was totally gorgeous."

"Hey, that sounds kind of nice, why are you so worked up about it?"

"Because everyone there was totally naked," I whispered. I could feel the heat of a blush rising up my face. "Guys and girls all sitting around like it was no big deal. And I was one of them."

"Well, you know you were kind of naked last night," she reminded me.

"Kind of naked?" I responded with a raise of my eyebrows.

Kenny began to chuckle, "Well the guys really were naked. I wonder who got volunteered to find their clothes?"

"Honestly, we should have stuck around to see who it was," I said snickering quietly.

"Are you two ready to go yet?" Rochelle said as she leaned over my shoulder and snatched a piece of bacon off my plate.

I looked up at her, "Where did you come from?" I asked. She was usually not so quiet.

"I wore my sneakers today," she said laughing.

"Let's go," I said, as I stood. "The stores await."

I knew our chatter and bursts of laughter could be heard around the corner. Heads turned to look as my friends and I made our way down the boardwalk.

"Let's go in there," said Kimi. "I've always wanted a cowboy hat."

I turned to see an extravagant display in the store window. There was a family of mannequins dressed in typical western attire, each of them sporting a cowboy hat.

Kimi pushed open the door and stepped inside without waiting to see if we were behind her.

"I guess we are going in," said Tammy.

The store had the largest number of hats I'd ever seen. There were large floppy sun hats and baseball hats with deer, tractor or hunting logos. Even darling little lace hats for babies. Covering the back wall were the cowboy hats; dark green, red with sequins, even pale blue ones.

Right in the middle was Kimi sporting a hot pink hat on her blond curls, a lasso swinging from her hands.

"Why don't you get a cowboy hat, Viv?" asked Rochelle.

"I don't know when I would ever wear it," I said surprised.

"Well, you should at least try one on. Look how cute Kimi looks."

"I guess it wouldn't hurt to try," I said, smiling. I picked up the hat closest to me and put it on. It was a white, straw hat with a tan leather band around the crown.

Walking up to me Kimi said, "No, you have to have it like this," pushing the hat down almost in my eyes. "It looks sexier that way."

"Ok," I said as I did a little hip sway down the aisle, turning back and giving Kimi the sexiest look I could. Laughter burst out of us like firecrackers.

A deep chuckle caused me to stop. My cheeks blossomed to a rosy shade of pink when I saw the old cowboy. A smile graced my face as I bobbed a quick curtsy. He tipped his hat, returned my smile and sauntered out of the store, the rhythmic tapping of his dusty boots fading on the boardwalk.

I slowly pulled the hat off my head and watched my friends move towards the door.

"Nice hat," Kimi said when I met them outside.

"Thanks," I said, smiling at her from under the brim.

"You going to be okay if we leave?" asked Rochelle

"Yeah, Jeff said he would be here at 1:00 and it is already 12:45 now. You guys go ahead. I know you have things you need to do. I'll be fine."

"Have fun," Kenny teased.

I waved goodbye as I watched my friends get in Kimi's sporty, red VW and drive away.

Now what? I wondered, as I made my way slowly to the corner. There was an old ranch truck sitting at the stop light. The driver, a young cowboy, nodded and smiled as I crossed the street.

I entered the park on the other side of the road, grateful for the ample trees, their broad branches casting patterns of shade on the sidewalk around me. A breeze picked up my hair, blowing it across my face and sticking to my gloss covered lips. I pulled it away and looked around, part of me hoping Jeff wouldn't come.

Spying a wooden bench in a secluded area of the park I headed over and sat down. The park was quiet, except for the gurgle of a small stream running on the far side of the path. A young couple was sharing an ice cream cone as they walked across the park. I pulled out my watch and saw that it was already after 1:00.

I wonder what's keeping him? I thought.

Reaching into my bag, I pulled out a book. Might as well do some reading while I wait.

The story was captivating and before long I was lost in its pages.

"Hey beautiful, what ya reading?" came a voice from behind me.

I spun around surprised to see Nic coming up behind me.

"I thought you were here with your friends?" he asked, his arms rested on the back of the bench right next to my shoulder. I had to tip my head back to see his face.

"I was, but they had to go back and Jeff was supposed to meet me here a while ago," I said.

Nic's eyes slowly met mine.

He winked and said "I was just about to go pick up some pictures at this photo gallery. You want to come?"

"I'd love to." I didn't see Nic smile as I bent down to put my book in my bag and picked up my hat off the bench at my side.

I felt a little uncertainty as I realized Jeff wasn't coming. I knew I wouldn't be doing anything with him again. I was elated at the idea of spending some alone time with Nic though.

The jingle of the bell alerted the clerk to our arrival.

"Hi, how can I help you?" she said.

"I need to pick up some pictures and I think she," Nic said looking at me, "just wants to look around."

I walked toward the gallery part of the photo store. The photos were marvelous. The colors were so vivid it almost felt I was standing in the meadow with the wildflowers. I felt I could reach out and touch the giant moose, or slide my feet into the cool water of the wide, slow moving river.

So engrossed in the amazing photos I didn't realize Nic was back until he bumped my shoulder with his arm.

"See anything you like, recently?" he said in a teasing voice.

I looked up to see him looking at me expectantly. I looked back at the photo on the wall and said "These photos are so astonishing, how does a person get shots like that. I wonder if it is luck or really skill. It's probably just a gift. I don't think I would ever be able to do anything like that."

I knew I was rambling but I couldn't help myself, I felt so stupid. I knew he was talking about seeing him the night before.

"I don't know about that, I just happen to have some photos that an amazing girl took just the other day. Maybe we should get some lunch and check them out."

I looked up at Nic, "That sounds like a nice idea."

Nic took my hand as we strolled on the boardwalk. It was more crowded out here than it had been in the park. The clomping of boots on the boards reminded me of the westerns I liked to watch with my dad.

"What are you in the mood for?" he asked.

I stopped, tipped my head to the side, in deep thought. "Pizza," I said with a grin,

"Sounds good to me, I know just the place."

The pizza parlor was pretty rustic looking but Nic promised it served the best in town.

A waitress led us to a corner booth where Nic sat across from me. The sultry sound of a guitar floated towards us from across the room. Instinctively I turned to see where it was coming from. On a dimly lit stage in the corner sat a young man. His blond hair hung over his face, his head bent as if hypnotized by his guitar.

Turning back I closed my eyes and dropped my head against the cushion on the back of the booth, feeling the music surround and fill me. My parents had given me my first guitar and it didn't take long before I was hooked. After mom died it became an escape. The jazz music of Miles Davis was my new favorite. I loved hearing him on his trumpet but his music had a way of coming alive through my guitar.

"So I take it you like jazz?" Nic murmured, his voice softly finding its way into my thoughts like a deep, rumbling purr.

"Ooooh yaaah. I love it," I said in a dreamy voice, still lost in the mood the guitar was spreading through the room. "Especially when I am stressed out, I just go play for a while and everything seems better."

"Well I'm afraid your pizza won't get better if you let it sit there too much longer."

"Oh, sorry,"

I opened my eyes to see Nic holding out a slice, cheese stretching from the pan. I leaned forward, letting my teeth sink into the thick, hot cheese.

We shared an enjoyable lunch. I kept expecting myself to get nervous and say something stupid, but it never happened. The longer we talked the more relaxed I became. He was so passionate about so many things. The sound of the few other customers in the restaurant faded into the background as I became lost in the blue of his eyes and the mesmerizing timbre of his voice.

All too soon it was time to go. Walking across the room with Nic, his hand at my back, I wondered why we weren't heading towards the door. I looked up at him questioningly.

"I want to meet the guitar player," was all he said.

I wondered what he had meant by that.

The guitarist's name was Mike. His family owned the restaurant and he came up most every summer to play. He had a studio in Denver where he did a lot of his writing and recording but he loved the inspiration he got from his hometown.

"I spend most mornings teaching guitar to local kids," Mike said.

"Would you mind if my friend Vivian here played something?" I heard Nic ask.

I started to shake my head no, "That's ok, I don't need to."

"I really want to hear you play." said Nic.

"Please," The exaggerated puppy dog look in his eyes was hard to resist

"I keep an extra one here in case some of my advanced students want to jam," Mike said handing me a guitar that had been leaning against the wall behind him.

I sat down and took a deep breath and focused on relaxing. I had felt such a connection with Nic that day and I so wanted to share this part of me with him. The rich sound flowed across the small stage as I strummed a few chords. I closed my eyes and saw myself in my room back home. It didn't take long for the music to flow from my fingers. I always loved being in that place, just me and my guitar and nothing else. The clinking of glasses and the quiet conversations slid away as my music filled the space. The poignant words drifted from my lips, unbidden, ending in a whisper.

The applause startled me. My eyelids fluttered open. Uncertainty filled me. Did he like it? A nod of thanks went out to the occupants in the room before I turned to return the guitar.

Mike placed it against the wall. "You can play with me anytime," he said generously.

Nic put his arm around my shoulder, pulling me close to his side.

"Amazing," he said softly, his breath a caress across my cheek.

"Thanks," I said as we headed outside.

"We never got to look at those photos," Nic said. "You want to go back to the park for a while."

Hours later we were still at the park looking at the pictures and talking. I was excited to see the meadows of wild flowers blossom in my photos. The blue green of the water shone sparkling and clear. My favorites were the ones I had taken of Nic, catching him unaware with a goofy look on his face. That one was definitely going to be framed and put on my dresser.

"What do you think of going on a bike ride?"

Nic's question came out of the blue. One minute we were discussing camera angles and now bicycles.

With Nic I never knew what to expect, that was one of the things I was beginning to find very attractive about him.

We ditched our gear in his jeep and headed off to a nearby bike rental shop.

Wobbling down the bike path I wondered if a person really could forget how to ride a bike. I didn't think it had been that long, but I just couldn't get the hang of it.

Nic was in front of me laughing so hard I thought the bike would tip over.

"Stop laughing," I cried as I poked him hard in the back. "You're going to make us crash."

That just made him laugh all the more.

Riding a tandem bike had been Nic's idea. It was hard just trying to stay up. His laughter wasn't helping. I enjoyed watching his muscles bulge and stretch under his t-shirt as he worked to keep the bike upright. Even if we never figured this out I was sure enjoying the view.

After what seemed like forever we finally got the hang of it and were cruising down the path, the wind blowing through our hair. We passed only a handful of bikers and joggers as we headed up the hill and into the shade of a grove of pine trees. Nic slowed the bike down to a stop and held it while I got off.

"I thought we could walk around a bit," he said.

We parked the bike on the edge of the path and began to wander into the trees. It felt cool under the tall branches and the smell was intoxicating. Nic put his arm around my shoulder and pulled me against him. It felt so right being here with him.

"Vivian."

I looked up and watched Nic as his face came closer. The touch of his lips was soft and warm.

"I'm glad you spent the afternoon with me," I heard him whisper, breaking the kiss as he leaned his forehead against mine.

"So am I."

The ride back to the jeep was filled with laughter. Nic made me take the front and I just couldn't get balanced. Mainly because I could feel Nic's eyes on me the whole time. He was so distracting with all his comments about fillies, and their long shapely legs. I don't know why he was stuck on that subject, we didn't see a single horse the entire way back.

Nic pulled into the Texaco station a few minutes after we returned to the jeep.

"I'll just be a minute," he said climbing out.

"Okay."

Nic's jeep smelled so much like him; pine and mint gum. I closed my eyes and relaxed, relishing the moment and let myself relive the afternoon.

"Hey, sleeping beauty, can you hand me my wallet?"

I opened my eyes to see Nic's face leaning in my window. I picked it up and turned to give it to him and found his lips on mine.

"Thanks."

I couldn't take my eyes off him as he walked away. Smiling secretly, I remembered seeing him not quite so dressed. His backside looked almost as good in pants as it did out of them.

"Nice hat," Tony said walking up to the jeep as Nic and I gathered our bags.

"Thanks."

"Hey, Vivian," I heard Jeff call.

"What do you want, Jeff?" I asked as Nic and Tony stepped around the back of the jeep.

"Didn't see you in town today, now I know why," he motioned to Nic.

"Nic gave me a ride home after you stood me up," I said reaching into the jeep to get my purse.

"Stood you up? I spent all afternoon looking for you."

"Hi Jeff, thanks for the great afternoon. We should do it again sometime."

I turned to see one of the waitresses he had been ogling the night of our date walk by.

"I don't think you spent any time looking for me but I don't care, I got a better offer." I pulled my hat down low, shut the door and walked away.

Nic grinned as I appeared at his side and took his hand.

Chapter 9

"Vivian, what are you doing after work?" Rochelle asked as she put away her cleaning supplies.

"I just want some food and go relax somewhere and not do anything," I said as I stuffed a pile of dirty bath towels in my cart.

The summer was almost over but the resort was busier than usual. A few of the housekeepers had left for the summer meaning more rooms to clean for those of us still here. I didn't mind too much but today had been a little long and I was in need of a break.

"Why don't we grab some food from the cafeteria and head over to the hot springs," suggested Rochelle.

"Skinny dipping?" I questioned, "You want to go skinny dipping?"

"No! Let's just go relax and eat," she said as a fleeting look of shock filled her eyes.

That sounded good to me. Girl time with Rochelle was just the thing I needed tonight. We had become good friends over the past few months and I was going to miss her when it came time to go home.

The line in the cafeteria was longer than usual. The room was filled with chaos and the noise was almost deafening. Jessie had outdone herself, a turkey dinner with all the fixings. We filled up the plastic containers Jessie had been kind enough to get us, with turkey, potatoes and gravy, a pile of mixed veggies and some rolls. As we were getting ready to leave Jessie came up with a takeout bag in her hand.

"What's this?" I asked.

"Just a little something sweet for the two of you," she said with a twinkle in her eyes.

Jessie had been that way all summer. Always giving out little extra treats or stopping to talk if she was out in the cafeteria. I could tell she really cared about the kids who worked there. It was nice to know that if I ever needed someone to talk to, she would be there. I gave her a quick hug and a thank you and we headed to the cooler to grab a couple water bottles.

"You girls should come sit by me and Alex," Kyle said as he filled his drink at the soda fountain.

"Thanks," I said, "but we're going somewhere quiet."

"Good luck," he said a little sarcastically as he headed back to his table.

We made our way to the door, the silence that greeted us was a welcome break after the din in the cafeteria. We walked back to our room enjoying the quiet. After quickly changing, we grabbed our towels and food and headed to the river.

The temperature was perfect for the almost fall evening. A soft breeze blew the red and gold leaves across our path, crushed beneath our feet.

I dug into the bag and pulled out two pumpkin cookies.

"Nothing wrong with dessert first, I'm too hungry to wait," I said taking a big bite of the soft, spicy cookie.

"So what are your plans when you get home?" I asked Rochelle, handing her the other.

"I am hoping to get into some drawing and painting classes," she responded taking the other cookie.

"You still haven't given me lessons," I teased.

"What I'd really love to do is go to Europe and study there for a year."

I smiled at the thought. I could just see her with her black bucket hat set jauntily atop her head, the Notre-Dame Cathedral taking shape on the canvas.

As we rounded the bend in the path the tranquil pool lay before us.

I slipped off my flip flops and stepped out of my shorts. I found the perfect spot and hurried into the water, immersing myself in its warmth. Breaking through the surface of the water I noticed Rochelle peering at me

"Now that feels marvelous," I said.

She sat down meticulously beside me.

"Think we can eat in here without drowning our food?" Rochelle asked.

I didn't realize she had grabbed our dinner and was sitting there holding it above the water.

"Sorry," I said as I sat up and carefully took mine, cradling it in my hands as the water flowed around my waist.

The deep green grass growing on the edge of the river swayed in the gentle breeze and the pungent smell of pine encased us in its arms. I felt so relaxed; I had no desire to get out.

With dinner finished I let myself sink deep into the warm water.

"Have you ever wondered why you have those dreams?"

Rochelle's question lifted through the silence that surrounded us.

"I haven't figured that out yet, even though I have thought a lot about it. They are all so different. Some are silly, like when I was young I dreamed that I had a strawberry ice cream cone. I ended up getting one the next day. Others are pretty intense. Did I ever tell you about the dream I had a month or so ago where I broke an arrow with my throat?"

"No way! Didn't that totally freak you out?"

"Ya, I'm glad that was just a dream," I said.

"Did you ever have a dream you wanted to come true?" she asked.

"There is this one; I have it at least once or twice a year. It is a simple yet stunning beach wedding."

"Oh, do tell," Rochelle said sliding close.

Whispering and giggling like silly school girls, I told her all about my dream wedding.

"Now that's the kind of dream you want to come true," Rochelle said with a sigh.

"I know."

A cool breeze began to blow through the tops of the trees. Dark clouds rolled towards us.

"I think we should be heading back," I said. "Looks like a storm."

We made our way to the edge of the pool and climbed out. Wrapped in our towels we slipped on our shoes and quickly gathered our clothes. Large raindrops splashed on the ground as we came out of the cover of the large pine trees. We darted down the path and rushed back to our room.

The last few weeks of the summer went by so fast. Nic spent long, frenzied evenings in the restaurant. It seemed everyone for miles around wanted one last meal at the resort before it closed. My days began early and didn't end until he was already waiting tables. I missed him.

Of course, we would hang out around the pool for an hour or two at the end of the day on one of his rare days off, but we were never alone. Our last night together Nic collapsed into the chair next to me before any of the girls could get it. I smiled at him; a smile that held none of the uncertainty that had been there at the beginning of the summer.

"Long day?" I asked quietly.

Nic nodded and laid his head back against the seat.

"I wish we could have gone skinny dipping again," Kimi said with a sigh. "That was so much fun, remember?"

"Of course we remember," Kenny replied. "It was only a few weeks ago."

"Yes, but I want to know who got volunteered to go get the clothes," I said looking at Nic, raising my eyebrows. The slight blush on Nic's neck and face gave him away.

I started to giggle, "Maybe I shouldn't have been in such a hurry to run away," I murmured to him, a little surprised at my cheeky flirting.

"I got picked because those three talk big, but they're just a bunch of chickens when they don't have clothes on." He glared at Kyle, Tony, and Alex.

"Whatever. Who's to say you didn't volunteer?" Tony joked, "It's your word against ours." They laughed, and Nic gave up, knowing there was no use arguing with them.

"Well, I don't mind, just so long as you don't make a habit of running around the woods naked. You never know what you might run into, chipmunks, a moose," I said with a smile at Nic.

"What's that silly grin on your face for, Tony?" Rochelle asked.

"I was just thinking about the night the skunk chased that guest all the way from the front lawn to the pool," he chuckled at the thought. "I've never seen anything so funny."

"I know!" Rochelle answered. "I thought for sure he'd get sprayed."

"Or fall in," Kenny added. "What about you, Viv? What's your favorite memory?"

"Definitely hiking to the lake," I said, looking right at Nic with a twinkle in my eye. His face lit up as I spoke. "It was so beautiful. And the company was nice too, I suppose." I did my best to wink at him, a skill I hadn't quite mastered. He winked back, no doubt hoping that I would never figure it out.

Conversation faded as the sun began its journey over the mountains.

A coolness in the air had settled over us. I didn't want to think about going back to my room. Most of my friends and I had to be to work early the next morning. There was more to do now that we were closing up and I know it would be a long day. Worst of all, Nic was leaving and I didn't want to miss any time with him.

We all hugged each other and said goodbye. I tried not to notice when Jackie hugged Nic, holding onto him for what seemed like far too long. I waited for him, not really sure if I should. I looked away and stared into the clear blue water of the pool.

"Can I walk you to your room?" Nic asked, coming up beside me.

"Sure," I said, excited that we would have some time alone.

As we walked, he wrapped his arm around my waist. "I'm going to miss you, you know," he said.

"You are?" I said in a voice full of relief. I was going to miss him terribly but it was so nice to hear the words and know he would be missing me as well.

"Of course I am. This has been one of the best summers of my life."

"I'm going to miss you too," I said. I looked at the ground, trying to hide the pink on my cheeks. "Make sure you send me those pictures. I don't want to forget what you look like," I teased.

"You won't forget." Nic said at last. "I'll make sure you won't."

Approaching my door Nic stopped and gathered me in his arms. I looked up searching his eyes for answers to my doubts. Did he really like me as much as I thought? Would he really miss me as much as I would him? His hands lightly caressed my cheeks. I could feel his warm breath on my face. He gently pressed his lips on mine. It was not a goodbye kiss. It felt more like a taste of something wondrous, a promise of what the future might hold.

"I'll write you," he said, his lips lingered near mine. "Write me back?"

I just looked into his beautiful blue eyes and nodded. I didn't say anything; I couldn't. He kissed my forehead, and left.

I walked in my room, the feel of Nic's kiss floating all around me.

"Wow Vivian," Rochelle teased. "Looks like you got a real 'goodnight' from Nic. You guys were out there for a while."

"Yeah. I guess I did," I said dreamily. I kept seeing the look in his eyes as I got ready for bed. Snuggled in the warmth of the blankets, I could still feel the heat on my cheeks where his hands had been.

Chapter 10

"Where am I?" I was so hot and could tell there was smoke everywhere. I could feel the heat of the fire and hear the sounds of trees popping but I couldn't open my eyes to see what was happening. I was in danger. Fear was growing inside me. I knew my friends were near but I couldn't see or hear them.

We've got to get out of this, I thought, feeling myself begin to panic. The heat and smoke were intensifying. I tried to open my eyes but the smoke was making it to painful. I could feel myself coughing and choking, I struggled to open my eyes again.

With great effort, I was finally able to pry my eyelids open. Everything was black or red. The images were blurry and I knew I had others I had to find and help before it was too late. I felt responsible for them.

"Help us! Anyone, please help!"

I could hear their cries and could tell they were panicking. I tried to make my way through the darkness towards their yelling, the smoke blinding in its thickness. It was so hot and I couldn't tell which way to go.

I closed my eyes hoping it was a dream and that it would all go away. When I opened them again the images were still there. I tried to make my way through the darkness towards the yelling. It was just so hot and the smoke so thick I could hardly breathe.

"Vivian!" It was Nic. I felt a powerful yet gentle hand grab mine.

I felt myself leave the ground, the icy water hitting me with stunning force. Nic was still there, beside me, lifting me. I felt myself being launched into the air, flying, then, landing in a pool of water well above him.

I wasn't sure what happened next. The image started to fade. I thought I heard someone scream, Nic!!!, as a huge burning log came crashing down over him.

Smoke seemed to still fill my lungs. Sitting up, I gasped, then started to cough and then to sob. I knew I was in bed in my dorm room at the resort, but just moments before I was in the middle of a raging fire. As I tried to quiet my crying I felt warm arms wrap around me.

"Another nightmare?" my sister Esther asked quietly.

I nodded.

"Have you had this one before?" she asked.

"No, there was a fire, smoke, I couldn't see anything. Nic was there."

"Were you okay?"

"I don't know it just ended."

"Do you want to talk about it?"

"Maybe tomorrow, I think I'll go sit outside for a while," I said.

I tiptoed out of the room and sat on the swing behind the dorm. The warmth of the blanket I had pulled off my bed was little comfort. The smell of the smoke and the crackling of the fire was still too intense in my mind. My eyes darted around and were drawn to the big stillness beyond the trees which seemed to float effortlessly across the shadowy sky to surround me.

Hoping to get my mind off the dream, my thoughts drifted back to the previous nine months when I was home. It had been hard to be there. Dad had a girlfriend. I hadn't seen him smile that much since mom was alive. I wanted to be happy for him but I felt like I was losing mom all over again and him too. Jillian was nice but I still felt awkward and uncomfortable around her. I was glad that school and work kept me busy.

Nic had written me, like he said and we talked on the phone every few weeks. He had even sent copies of the pictures he had promised. I spent hours looking at all the photos of him that I had taken. He was so dreamy. I still wondered what he liked in me?

"Hey, Vivian are you going to work today or just sit on the patio daydreaming?" Tammy hollered on her way to breakfast.

My eyes flew open startled with the realization that I had fallen asleep. I jumped up and hurried inside.

"Where have you been, Viv?" asked Esther who was ready to leave.

"I was just outside for a while and lost track of time."

"You better hurry if you don't want to be late," she said as she left the room.

Throwing the blanket on my bed in a heap, I grabbed my clothes and headed to the bathroom for a quick shower.

Hurrying through the breakfast line I quickly found a seat by Rochelle and ate my yogurt and bagel.

"Esther said to tell you she would meet you here for lunch. She seemed a little anxious to get to work," Rochelle said. "What took you so long?"

"I couldn't sleep and went outside for a while. I must have dozed off or something."

"Dreaming about Nic, I bet," she said grinning. "You didn't forget that he was coming today did you?"

"No, that's all I've been able to think about for days," I said. I was eager to see him and talk to him but the dream left me unsettled. Some of my dreams had come true and I didn't want to live through this one.

"Are you looking forward to working in the main lodge this year," Rochelle asked as we walked down the hall after breakfast.

"I think so," I said as I grabbed my cart and headed to my first room. "See you at lunch."

The morning went by quickly; even making the swan towels was a breeze this summer. I only had to make a few before I remembered how to do it.

"Are you sure you want to do housekeeping again this year?" Kenny had questioned me on my first day back.

"Yes, I like the routine and I get to make swans," I said grinning.

Moving around to make the other side of the bed I glanced out the window and saw Nic walking across the parking lot towards the lodge.

I hurried over to the window to get a better look, a better look at him sharing a big hug and kiss with Jackie! A gasp broke from me as I stared at the scene in front of me. Not wanting to believe what I was seeing. I quickly turned away from the window and threw the pillow I had been holding across the room. I wanted to be the one down there wrapped in his arms with his lips on mine.

Lunch with the girls was a challenge. Trying to keep my mind off Nic and hiding my feelings was stressful. I just didn't think I could handle their teasing or prying questions just yet. I was glad Nic wasn't there. I didn't know what I was going to say to him, first the dream and now the kissing.

The rest of the afternoon had me deep in thought. It was time to go back to my dorm and I didn't even remember cleaning the last 4 rooms. I kept going over in my mind the scene of Jackie in Nic's arms. I knew I was probably blowing it way out of proportion but I just couldn't help it. I really needed to talk to someone.

I wonder if Jessie would have time to talk tonight, I thought.

The rest of the evening I intentionally avoided the places that I knew Nic might be. He didn't have to work that night and so that made staying out of his way a bit tricky.

The sun had dipped low behind the mountains by the time I headed off to find Jessie. The paved path from the dorms gave way to a trail that led to a group of small cabins. Jessie's was the last cabin before the trail turned to head towards the resort. As I approached I saw her lying in a hammock strung from two supports on her porch reading a book. I didn't want to interrupt so I turned to leave.

"Where you off to, Vivian?" Miss Jessie called as she closed her book and climbed out of the hammock.

"I was hoping to be able to talk to you about something but I didn't want to interrupt," I said.

"Come sit here," she said, patting a cushioned chair.

The trail that led to her porch created clouds of dust with each step. I was hoping Jessie would help me get rid of the dust clouds that were floating around in my head.

"What's on your mind?" she asked as she sat in the matching striped chair next to me, leaned back and put her feet up on the railing. The gentle movement of the hammock behind her, in the deepening night sky, sent soft waves of peace over me.

"I have these dreams," I said. "They seem so real but I can never tell who is in them. The faces are fuzzy and unclear. Sometimes they are really short and happen during the day and other times I dream all night."

"So have you had one recently?" she asked.

"Yes, I had one early this morning. It really scared me."

"So what happened this time?" Jessie asked

Slipping out of my shoes I pulled my feet up on the chair and wrapped my arms around my legs. I then told Jessie about my dream.

"I knew it was Nic because I recognized his voice. But the awful thing was I don't want Nic to die," I said.

Jessie put her feet down and turned her chair to face me.

"Just because you see something in a dream doesn't mean it is going to happen. There are all sorts of reasons why we dream."

My eyes wandered across the porch; crowded with terra cotta pots teeming with herbs. Tucked between a brightly painted pot and the railing was a small red wagon boasting its own assortment of draping plants.

"But I have had dreams that actually happened," I said, my voice fading as I was drawn back to the dream I'd had when I was 13.

It was a dark and cold. The light of a small lamp cast an eerie glow across the room, coming to rest on the solitary bed. A woman lay there, her chest slowly rising and falling as she slept. On her pillow were tufts of long, dark hair rubbed off as she moved in the night. Wires and tubes lay carefully draped across the blankets connecting boxes of flashing lights and a discord of soft, high pitched beeps to the pale, almost translucent arm lying draped off the edge of the bed.

The picture in my mind faded as the porch light began to flicker, disturbing the collection of moths with an eruption of fluttery wings, only to return to merge with the soft light once more. I stretched my legs, my foot sliding slowly, back and forth on the baluster.

"If it is a dream about a future event, just you knowing about it gives you the chance to make it different," Jessie said

"You really think it could be changed?"

"Vivian, I don't believe our lives are set in stone. I believe anything can be changed, even dreams."

So, do you think I should tell Nic about it?"

"What do you think?" Jessie responded, her eyes searching mine as if searching for an answer I wasn't ready to vocalize.

"Well, if I do maybe he can help me change it?" I said a little hesitantly.

"That's something to think about, I'd say," Jessie said.

"I would like to talk to Nic but I saw him hugging and kissing Jackie today."

"Are you sure it was Nic doing the hugging and kissing?" Jessie asked leaning back in her chair and studying me.

"I don't know. I only saw them for a minute before turning away. I guess it could have been Jackie."

Across the darkness came a low, tranquil tone. The note stirred emotions deep inside. It was the first time I had heard Kyle play that summer. It was a haunting, mournful yet beautiful melody. I closed my eyes and let the quiet song of the night soothe my troubled mind. As the last note faded into the night I turned to Jessie.

"That was divine," I whispered.

We sat there, felt the deep velvet night surround us, reveled in the peace of it. The quiet was interrupted by the distant hoot of an owl.

"It's getting late, I should probably go," I said as I leaned over and slipped on my shoes.

"What are you going to do about Nic?" Jessie asked.

"I guess I need to tell him," I said softly.

Jessie stood, wrapped me in a tender hug.

"Thanks," I said as I stepped out of her arms and headed out into the darkness.

It was after midnight when I got back to my room. I felt a lot better after talking to Miss Jessie, but I was still unsure of when I would talk to Nic. I didn't see him at all the next few days. Both Kenny and Rochelle told me that Nic had stopped by several times looking for me but I had extra to do at work and kept missing him.

Today had been just terrible, we were short staffed because some kids got food poisoning in town and couldn't work. I had extra rooms to get done and I had been running all day. I was glad the day was ending, after the awful dream and the crazy last few days I was feeling exhausted. I slipped into my pjs, climbed into bed, turned off the lamp and settled down for some much needed sleep.

Chapter 11

I gasped, with the speed of a runaway freight train, my upper body shot up off the pillow. The room was dark, but my eyes were wide open. Breathing heavily I tried to force the images out of my mind. The alarm clock on the nightstand read 3:32 am. I rubbed my hands over my face, as if to scrub off the taint that the dream had left me with.

"You okay?" Esther asked with a yawn. I could hear her rustling in her sheets, and instantly felt guilty for waking her up.

"Yeah, I'm fine," I said, trying to slow down my breathing. "I just had a bad dream is all."

"Another one? You seem to be having a lot more recently. What was it about this time?" Esther asked sleepily.

"I was in some room," I began. "I've never seen it before, but I know it was mine. His and mine. There he was on the floor. I just stood there, looking at him. He wasn't moving, just lying there. It felt like walking through tar as I made my way across the room. I didn't see any blood. But the room was in shadows, heavy drapes had been pulled over the windows. I reached out to touch his arm. It was cold, like 'dead' cold."

I shivered despite the heat of the room and pulled my blankets tighter around me. I heard Esther drag herself out of bed. Her feet padded across the floor until she reached me. She sat down on the edge of my bed and put a comforting arm around my shoulder.

"It was just a bad dream, Vivian," she said. "It'll be okay." I tensed, feeling a little brushed off especially since Esther knew all about my dreams.

"Yeah, thanks Esther," I said. But the horror I had felt in the dream still hadn't gone, and I was almost certain that it wouldn't be okay. Esther stood up and went back to her bed.

"I'm sorry I woke you up," I whispered.

"It's okay," Esther answered. A fan clicked on by Esther's bed, filling the room with a constant, gentle whirring.

"It'll be okay. It'll be okay," I whispered to myself, as I laid my head back down on the pillow. "It'll be okay."

The warm sunlight streaming in my room felt comforting after the awful night I had just had. I rolled over and saw Esther's bed made up neatly. It must be later than I thought. I reached over and picked up my clock. 9:04. Realization dawned on me, I needed to catch the bus by 10:00 if I wanted a ride to the trail head. I leaned over and picked up my dream notebook, turned to a blank page and quickly wrote "Dead husband". Then tossed it carelessly back on the dresser. I slipped out of bed, gathered my clothes and headed to the bathroom for a quick shower.

With my brown hair pulled up, out of the way with an elastic, I slung my backpack over my shoulder and hurried out to catch the bus to the lake. My camera, some extra 35mm film and a few snacks I had taken from the cafeteria the night before were inside my pack, as well as a canteen of water.

"The bus leaves at two," the driver said as passengers began to exit, after our short drive to the trail.

A colorful array of flowers beckoned me as I stepped off the bus. My camera hung around my neck and I threw my pack on my back. My tan hiking boots stirred up the dust on the path. It meandered through the tall grass to a small meadow nestled beneath the grandeur of the mountains, creating a backdrop for the rainbow of colors below. I detoured off, wandered among the flowers wondering where to begin. A bouquet of red paintbrush called to me. Crouching I snapped a few frames. The bluebells, buttercups and sunflowers were a painting by Monet, a blending of shades and textures.

I left the colorful splendor behind. The sound of water lapping against the shore and the call of birds summoned me on. The lake was clear, translucent and shimmered in the afternoon sun. A breeze blew my now loose hair across my face. The elastic stretched around my wrist. I closed my eyes and let the wind and sun play.

A large fallen log lay stretched across the beach, resting partially in the water. My gray socks were quickly stuffed in my boots and left lying in the shade. I gingerly made my way across the rocks and sand to the water. My foot hung apprehensively for a moment before daring to plunge into the icy water. I stepped in further, the waves sent a chill surging up and down my legs.

The laughter of nearby children drew my attention as they splashed and played. I carefully centered their frolicking bodies in my lens and took four shots in rapid succession.

I made my way back to the log and sat back letting my feet dry. A young couple sat on an air mattress, floating casually around the dock. I focused in on an old fisherman, asleep in his chair, his hat pulled over his eyes and his line bobbing in the water. He reminded me a little of my granddad.

I sat and watched him while I ate my lunch. The fishing pole began to move wildly. Startled, the fisherman jerked awake and struggled to his feet, hands searching for the pole that had been knocked over in his hurry. The top of the pole teetered on a nearby branch. The fish thrashed wildly, dragging the pole closer to the water. The old man's foot landed just below the reel, holding it long enough for him to keep it from swimming away. Slowly reeling in the line, the fish continued its struggle for freedom. The bend in the rod was evidence of the fight. Only one could claim victory. The line went still, the fish hung lifeless above the water.

What a story my pictures would tell, I thought as I lowered my camera.

"How was the lake?" Esther asked as I came in the room, feeling hot and sticky.

I was glad to be back and looking forward to a long, cool shower. The bus ride had been longer than it should have because of all the tourists stopping in the middle of the road to take pictures.

"It was amazing," I said. "Let me get cleaned up and I'll tell you about it."

The cool water felt like a waterfall running down my back. It was good to be clean again.

"Vivian, are you almost done? Nic is here and wants to talk to you," Kennedy hollered into the bathroom.

"Not quite, I'm still going to be a while," I called. I could have hurried but looking like a drowned rat wasn't really the way I wanted him to see me.

"He has to be to work in 10 minutes and was wondering if you could meet him at the restaurant around 11:00 when his shift ends."

Memories of the dream started to fly through my mind. Being with Nic is something I wanted, but I was so afraid of something terrible happening to him.

"I don't know, I've had a long day. Just tell him I will see him tomorrow after work."

"I'll tell him but I don't think he is going to like it," said Kenny.

I didn't like it either but what was I supposed to say. "Oh by the way Nic, I dreamed of a dead guy in my room and I'm afraid it's you so I better not see you anymore, and don't forget you died in a fire too." He would think I am such a dork.

The following evening arrived faster than I expected. My steps slowing as I made my way up the stairs to the restaurant.

"Vivian!" said Nic his eyes lit up at the sight of me. "Where have you been? I've been looking for you since I got here," he said as his arms reached around me

"Nic," said Alex "let's go."

Nic looked down at me still held in his arms. "My shift started like five minutes ago but I want to talk. Would you meet me here at 11 when it's over?"

Pausing, I shake my head slowly, "I don't know, I'll try. You better go so you're not late for work." I force myself to pull out of his arms and slowly walk away. I glance over my shoulder to see Nic look at me with a puzzled expression on his face. I chided myself for being so scared and nervous. It's just Nic. He really did seem happy to see you, I lectured myself as I turned and walked back down the stairs.

"What a great party," Kimi said to me and Esther, the next evening, as the three of us wandered around the pool. "It has all the party perks, hot guys, door prizes and plenty of delicious looking pastries."

Speaking of hot guys, I hadn't seen Nic at all that day. I knew he was here and that he deserved an explanation for my actions yesterday. It had been unkind of me to just walk away like that. I was going to meet him last night to explain but I ended up falling asleep.

"I am going to find Nic," I said. "I'll see you two later."

I strolled between bikini clad girls and guys in swim trunks, but no Nic.

Just my luck, he's probably still working, I thought as I stepped carefully along the perimeter of the pool.

"Watch out!"

I turned and discovered a very muscular back hit my shoulder, knock me off balance and sent me, arms flailing, into the pool below. Sundress and all.

Sputtering I came to the surface. Blood rushed to my face as I looked up and saw everyone staring. There I stood in four feet of water, sopping wet and out of breath.

"Are you alright?" Tony asked. "I'm so sorry, someone bumped me."

"Ya I'm fine," I said. I waved away his outstretched hand and made my way to the steps and climbed out.

Esther hurried over with a towel. I took it and pulled it around my shoulders.

"Are you ok?" she asked.

"Yes, just feeling a little stupid. I'm going to go change. I'll see you later."

A trail of wet footprints followed me down the road. Water dripped and tickled down my legs. I reached back, clutched the back of my dress and wrung it out. A puddle of water collected at my feet.

"What happened to you?"

I looked up to see Nic trying hard not to laugh. His eyes twinkled with amusement.

"Sure, you can laugh, you weren't the one who was shoved in the pool," my own smile spreading across my face.

Nic took my arm and down the road we went, serenaded by the squishing of my flip flops.

We ended up on the patio by my dorm. The bench swing was warm against my chilled thighs. My dress stuck to my back causing me to shift uncomfortably on the seat. It was painfully obvious how nervous I was now that I was alone with Nic.

I pushed off and the swing began to move. I kept my head down, concentrating on pushing the swing, back and forth.

"I get the feeling you have been avoiding me since I got back," Nic said with a little nudge on my arm.

"A little and I'm sorry about that. It wasn't very nice of me," I said glancing at Nic and then looking out at the trees just beyond the patio.

"Why? Does it have anything to do with Jackie? Tammy told me that you saw her kiss me the day I got here."

"I did," I said with a slow nod. "And I guess it made me jealous."

"She's just a friend. She was excited because she had been offered a job at the university in our town and got a little carried away when she came to tell me," Nic said.

"I guess I thought it was something more than that."

"There's something else going on," Nic said as he placed his fingers under my chin and turned my head towards him. "I can see it in your eyes. Won't you tell me?"

My eyes closed, unsure of where to begin. With a deep breath I dove into my explanation.

"Ever since I was little I've been having dreams. I would even have 'episodes' during the day. Sometimes they are ok but sometimes they are kind of scary. I've had some that have come true."

I paused too fearful to continue.

"Viv, what is it?" Nic's deep, velvety voice wrapped around me, soothing my fear and uncertainty.

"I've never told anyone, but I dreamed about my mom once when I was about 13."

"I'm guessing it wasn't a good dream," Nic said softly.

I shook my head. Tears began to run down my cheeks. "I dreamed she died," I whispered.

Nic pulled me onto his lap, wrapped me in his arms and just held me.

Chapter 12

Sprawled on my bed I stared unseeing out the window. My dream notebook lay open beside me. My mind kept drifting back to Nic and our conversation the night before. I still couldn't believe what I'd told him. It just felt right. I was still confused about the dreams and how it could possibly hurt Nic. The doubt hanging in the back of my mind was hard to ignore. What if I let myself be with him more and something happened? I could never forgive myself. Better to just stay away and have him safe, I justified.

I heard voices and laughter coming down the hall. Sitting up, I closed my notebook and stuffed it in the top drawer of my dresser.

Esther came in and flopped on her bed.

We shared a small dorm room that summer. Just big enough for two twin beds and two matching dressers. There was space at the end of the room for a couple of chairs and a tall dresser next to the window.

"Vivian, how about going on a trail ride with Ben, Rochelle, Kyle and I?" Esther asked.

"I don't know," I replied "It seems a little hot to be out on a horse all day." My nerves began to do a little dance in my stomach. It had been years since I'd been on a horse.

"It's only for a few hours and Ben said the trail we are going to is in a forest," she said. "All you've been doing is working and hanging out here in our room. That's no way to spend a summer."

"I know, I'm sorry. I was the one who talked you into coming and now I'm not being any fun. Getting out would probably be a good idea. You just can't laugh when I get on my horse."

"It was so funny seeing you try to get on the last horse you rode, or tried to ride I should say," Esther said laughing.

The next morning turned out to be surprisingly cool so I grabbed my jacket on the way to breakfast. I glanced around the cafeteria as I entered and saw Esther and Ben sitting next to each other at a table by the window. Picking up a plate of scrambled eggs and toast I hurried over.

"Morning," said Esther as I sat down beside her. "Good news and bad news. Which one first?" she asked me.

I said bad news just to get it over with.

"Rochelle and Kyle aren't coming. They were called in to work," she said

"Well, what's the good news then?" I asked.

"This seat saved for anyone?"

I glanced up to see Nic standing across from me nodding to the chair.

"Of course not," I said.

"We were saving it for you," Esther said with a smirk. Then, looking at me, she said, "there's the good news. Nic is coming."

"Great," I said.

I ended up sitting in the back with Nic. I stayed close to the door, pretending to look at the scenery as we drove. I couldn't keep myself from glancing at him out of the corner of my eye. Wishing he would say something, at the same time glad that he didn't. I knew he was curious after last night but I didn't know what to say.

Ben pulled his car into a small gravel parking area adjacent to a small cabin. As we all climbed out, an older woman in wranglers and a plaid shirt came out to greet us. The spurs on her boots jangled as she walked. She introduced herself as Meg.

She put her tan cowboy hat low on her head, her long blond braid hanging down her back, and led us up the small incline to the corral. There were at least ten horses standing next to the fence all saddled and ready for riders. A beautiful, dark brown mare whinnied and shook her head as I came near.

"You can pet her," Meg said as she sauntered over towards me.

Reaching out tentatively I stroked the mare's soft nose.

"She seems gentle," I said admiring the graceful looking animal.

"Very," Meg said resting her foot on the bottom fence rail. "Would you like to ride her?"

I nodded as I rubbed the mare's soft fur. The butterflies that had taken flight in my stomach calmed a little.

Meg climbed over the fence and led out the mare. Two brown horses were next. Quarter horses she said. They were for Ben and Esther. Nic asked to ride a beautiful high spirited appaloosa.

Getting into the saddle took a few tries but once I was settled the butterflies that had started up again finally landed.

Once we were ready we moved down the trail. I soon realized that I didn't need to worry about Esther's lack of experience; she had ridden fewer times than I had. Ben was attentive and knew what he was doing. I soon felt comfortable leaving her in his capable hands. Nic handled his frisky, black and white spotted horse with relaxed confidence.

The path was so narrow we had to ride in single file for the first few miles. It was peaceful as the horses rambled along the trail, winding through pine trees, aspen groves and wild roses. We had been steadily climbing, but up ahead I could see a break in the trees. A beautiful meadow was laid out before us. The path widened and Ben nudged his horse up next to Esther. I smiled as I watched my little sister. He kept close to her, their legs almost touching as they rode side by side. Esther's face was glowing, and her smile didn't waver for a second.

I was feeling more at ease with Nic, too, but I still tried my best not to look over at him as he urged his horse up next to mine.

"Should we stop and stretch for a minute?" Ben said finally. We had been riding for almost an hour and every bouncing step the horse took reminded me that my bladder was full. We stopped by a mossy pond where the horses could drink and rest. At the first opportunity, I headed off into the trees.

"I'll be right back," I told Esther.

She started laughing at something Ben said and I guessed that she hadn't even noticed I was leaving. I didn't want to go too far into the woods, but the last thing I wanted was for Nic to stumble across me. I went a comfortable distance and then added a few extra yards to be safe.

I had always hated using the bathroom in the woods, so it took me a few minutes to convince myself that it was actually worth it. As I crouched in the underbrush, I heard a scuffling sound nearby. Freaking out I hurriedly finished and looked around frantically, just knowing that Nic was going to come into view any second. But, much to my surprise, it wasn't Nic. It was a huge, musty bull moose, his antlers shifting as he pushed his nose around in the grass. He stood over six feet tall and was about 20 feet away. A harsh gasp flew unrestricted from my lungs. The moose's head shot up and I realized my mistake. In one quick movement I straightened up and pulled up my pants, covering up as best I could without alarming it further.

"Nic!" I whispered frantically. I knew the chances that he could hear me were thin, but I didn't care. "Nic!" I said, a bit louder this time, my heart pounding in my chest. By then the moose was looking right at me, and he didn't look pleased as he slowly advanced in my direction.

"Nic!"

"Vivian?" I heard him whisper. His footsteps were coming closer, crunching lightly on fallen leaves. The moose, too, kept moving closer.

"Help!" I breathed.

"It's okay," he said, coming up next to me. "Just take a few steps back, slowly." He gently took my arm to guide me backwards.

"Keep your head down a little bit and we'll just try to blend in with the trees, okay?"

"Okay," I said as I watched the leaves and dirt appear with each step back. I kept moving, wondering if the moose was still following but not brave enough to check.

"Alright Vivian," Nic said finally, "you're safe."

Embarrassed, I looked up at Nic. We had emerged from the trees and were standing on the far side of the pond. "Thanks," I said quietly.

"Of course. It's not every day I get to save a damsel in distress." Again, he looked at me with that dazzling smile that had first caught my attention last summer.

"Well, thanks," I stammered. I turned to leave, but I stopped when I saw Esther and Ben across the pond. They were just starting to climb back onto their horses. I turned back to Nic. "Please don't tell them about this."

"Of course not," he answered, but as I walked away I thought I heard him stifle a laugh. I cringed and hurried to my horse, petting her for a moment before I mounted. I peeked over at Nic as he rode up and mouthed "thank you." He gave me a slight nod and gestured me to move ahead on the trail.

As we rode, I tried to keep in conversation with Esther and Ben, but they were too engrossed in each other. Everything I said seemed to spark another conversation about something they had in common. Eventually I gave up and just enjoyed the feel of the horse under me and the view of the valley around me. I surveyed the near perfect scene before me with its wide expanse of soft green grass, edged by tall trees and interrupted by little marshes. In the summer sun, with a light breeze blowing through, I felt nature's calm penetrate deep inside.

As the path approached a more heavily wooded area, my mare trotted off to a patch of tall grass to eat. I tried to nudge her forward and catch up with Esther and Ben but she was determined to get her fill before moving on. The others got farther and farther ahead and soon Nic had passed me. He looked back and slowed his horse to a casual walk. Surrounded by the trees, sitting on his proud black and white stallion with his back to me, he was exactly as I had described him in my notebook.

"Isn't it beautiful out here?" Nic said once we were on our way again. Esther and Ben were long out of earshot by now, and we were as good as alone.

"It's incredible," I replied. "I wish it could be like this all the time."

"Me too," he paused. "It reminds me of being at the lake with you."

"That was beautiful too," I answered.

"We should go back there again," Nic told me, but I could tell he wasn't talking about the lake.

"Nic, I..."

"Hey, you two coming or what," Ben yelled.

Nic looked over at me expectantly.

"Nothing," I said as I nudged my horse forward.

Chapter 13

What is that smell? I thought as I carried the swan towel into the bathroom. I stood there a little shocked at what lay before me. Someone had been extremely drunk or violently ill and ended up doing it all over the floor. It looked as if they had tried to clean it up, but everything was sticky and the smell was almost too strong to bear. I pulled my shirt up over my nose and turned on the fan hoping to make the air somewhat breathable while I cleaned. As I caught the sight of my arm—covered to the elbow with a yellow rubber glove—another image filled my mind.

I was still kneeling, still on the floor in front of a toilet, scrubbing the most disgusting gas station bathroom I had ever seen. I was absolutely grossed out, and feeling absolutely hopeless. I knew I had no choice but to be there and I knew that the next day and the next day after that would be exactly the same. It seemed as if the grimy, sticky walls were closing in on me.

Before the image faded, I remembered the dream I had a week ago of the man lying dead on my bedroom floor.

All these dreams of late left me feeling hopeless. Were they my future? Was that what my life was going to be like? My eyes stung with tears; but I'd done too much crying lately and I fought them. With a knot in my stomach and tears constantly welling in my eyes, I finished cleaning and went back to the cart in the hallway.

Tammy was at the cart too, loading up dirty towels and sheets to take to the laundry room. I added mine to the pile and wiped my eyes on the sleeve of my shirt.

"You okay?" she asked tenderly.

"Yeah, I'm fine," I said. "The fumes from the cleaners are just getting to me," I lied.

"Ya. Right," she raised her eyebrow. "What's wrong?"

"I just had another one of my daydreams," I said, not sure what to call it. Words like "vision" and "premonition" would sound too ridiculous. "I was stuck cleaning this disgusting bathroom. It looked like someone had gone the bathroom all over the floor. It was even up on the walls. The smell was gruesome. I knew no matter how clean I got it I would just have to come back the next day and do it all over again." My gut wrenched again.

"Wow," Tammy laughed. "I think you need another day off."

"What?" I answered, stunned by her reaction. What was there to laugh about?

"I mean, I don't particularly love cleaning bathrooms either, but I don't have nightmares about it." She kept laughing as we pushed the cart to the next cluster of rooms. I grabbed a pile of towels and pushed a door open. As she walked into the room across the hall she called, "If the shower curtain starts attacking, yell for me okay?"

I didn't say anything—I didn't want her to know how hurt I was.

"I know you've been reconsidering, but think about it, Vivian," Esther warned after I told her what I had seen. "What if Nic was the man lying dead on the floor? What if Nic was the reason you had to get a job scrubbing a gas station toilet to make enough money to survive?"

"It might not have been him," I argued. "I never saw his face, it could have been anyone."

"I don't think so," Esther asserted. "You've been having more and more dreams since you met him. This, the fire, the man on the horse. That one has already come true—and it was Nic."

I couldn't deny that. Every day it seemed more and more likely that these dreams really were about Nic, but I wanted desperately to believe that they weren't.

"I know you like him, Vivian," Esther put her hand on my shoulder as we sat next to each other on my bed. "But I think you need to let it go. I can't see it going anywhere good...and neither can you." I knew her advice made sense, but I couldn't help but rationalize that she was biased; Ben had been neglecting her the last few days and she was sure he was spending time with someone else. If I decided to give things with Nic a try, she would be alone for the rest of the summer. I didn't want to believe that my sister would do that to me—but I also didn't want to believe that a relationship with Nic was impossible.

My mood steadily declined over the next few days as I puzzled over what to do. I started going straight back to my room after dinner instead of going to the pool or walked around the grounds aimlessly. I stopped smiling at Nic when we passed each other at work, feeling the guilt grow every time I did. His face grew more confused every time.

"What can we do to make you feel better?" Kenny asked. "There's got to be something." She and Rochelle sat across from me on the floor in their room, their eyes pleading.

"I don't know," I said honestly. "I'm just so stressed about Nic—I can't figure out what to do."

"You need to stop thinking about it," Rochelle advised. "Find a way to distract yourself."

"I've tried!" I moaned. "I keep busy all day with work; I do my best not to run into him. I've even started reading the tourist brochures in the lobby. " The girls cringed.

"How about we go skinny dipping?" Kenny said, her eyes glittering. "I think it's the perfect thing!"

"Right now?" I asked.

"Yeah, right now."

I sat looking at them for a moment, trying to think of an excuse. But the more I thought about it, I realized that they were right. It was the perfect thing.

"Okay," I said finally. "Let's go."

The three of us tiptoed out of the building, not even bothering to change into our swimsuits, and hurried down the path to the hot springs. I wasn't shy this time as I flung my clothes onto the big rock and jumped into the prickly-hot water. We stayed in until our fingers and toes were wrinkled. It was nice not thinking about Nic for a while.

Walking back to the cabin, I regretted not wearing a swimsuit. My legs were chafing on my jeans and my hair was dripping water down my t-shirt. "It's kind of cold out," I said as my teeth chattered.

"It must be getting ready to rain or something," Kenny suggested. "It's never this cold out this time of year."

As we rounded the last curve on the path, I saw Nic standing outside the cabin door.

"What is he doing here?" I breathed, shivering even more.

"My guess is, he's here to talk to you," Rochelle answered, chastising me. "He's been really patient, Vivian. I think you owe him an explanation, you know?"

"I know," I said. And I did know—I just wasn't sure how much I should tell him.

"We'll see you inside," Kenny said, and they hurried in ahead of me, leaving me alone with Nic.

"Hey," I said. It was all I could manage.

"Hey." His eyes were downcast, surrounded by dark circles. "I haven't seen you around much lately."

"I know. I'm sorry."

"What's going on? I thought you said we could at least be friends. You said that's what you wanted."

"I know I did, I just…" I wrapped my arms around my stomach.

"I don't understand," he said, growing agitated. "Why won't you tell me what's wrong? I've been going out of my mind trying to figure it out."

"Nic, I—"

"I've asked all your friends, I've asked your sister, and none of them can give me a good explanation. I even asked Jessie."

"And what did she say?" I asked, curious to hear.

"She said you're afraid for me," he said discouragingly. "That you want to protect me, and you think that staying away from me is the best way to do that."

"Well, what if she's right?" I answered. I always knew Jessie could see right to the heart of things. Just like my mother.

"I think that's the worst excuse I've ever heard." His words cut deep as I realized what he meant. "If you don't want to be with me, Vivian, just say it to my face. Because as far as I'm concerned, that's the only reason for us not to be together." Reaching up he ran his hands roughly through his hair. His eyes looked full of hurt. I had been leaving him hanging for too long.

"I want to be with you, Nic. I really want to be with you!" I cried. "I've been scared—but if you're not scared, then it's okay. I love you, Nic." I didn't realize until I saw him walking away that I hadn't said any of it out loud.

I didn't go inside. I must have wandered around for an hour, replaying the whole scene in my head. Why do I always keep my feelings hidden? It would have been so easy just to come out and say what I felt. He understood when I told him about my mom. Why do I always get scared?

Without thinking about it, I wandered into Jessie's kitchen. There were only a couple of people left doing dishes, it being so late, but Jessie was nowhere to be seen.

"I think she went out to the parking lot." A scruffy-chinned guy said. "A friend of hers was supposed to be coming tonight."

"Oh," I said in a daze. "Thanks."

He looked at me like one would a lost child. "Do you want me to help you find her?" he asked.

"No," I said, forcing myself into the present. "I can find her." I left the kitchen not really intending to find her at all. But I wasn't ready to go back to my room—I couldn't face Kenny and Rochelle yet—so the parking lot seemed like the best alternative. I came out of the building just in time to see Jessie approach a young couple and fling one arm around each of their necks. "I'm so happy you're here!" she exclaimed "It's been too long." As she pulled away, she saw me standing on the curb.

"Vivian!" she smiled. "Come here, come here! Come meet my friends." Reluctantly, I obeyed. "Vivian, I'd like you to meet Tom and Elsie Campbell," she said. I could hear in her voice how much she cared for them.

"Tom, Elsie—this is Vivian."

"Nic's Vivian?" Elsie said excitement in her eyes. As she looked me up and down I found myself feeling like a mannequin in a store window.

"You know Nic?" I asked, feeling a wave of shame sweep over me. I could only imagine what he had told them about me.

"Of course!" Jessie explained. "They were here last summer. I introduced Nic to them during dinner one night."

"Nic told us a lot about you," Elsie smiled. "You're just as pretty as he said."

Tom rolled his eyes teasingly as I blushed. "Sorry, Vivian, this girl couldn't keep a secret if her life depended on it." He nudged her affectionately, and they exchanged the same knowing look.

After we helped Tom and Elsie get settled into their room, Jessie linked her arm in mine, and I was tempted to lay my head on her shoulder. The lavender oil she wore reminded me of the dried lavender my mom kept around the house. I just inhaled deeply and then we walked back to the kitchen. The resort was so quiet I could have leaned in and heard people breathing through the walls if I stopped. The halls were dimly lit, and I was comforted listening to our feet padding on the carpet.

"Now," Jessie said, "tell me what happened, the whole story this time."

I felt braver with her next to me, like I could tell her anything and everything. I told her about the dreams, the visions, everything that had happened since I had been to her cabin. I thought it must all be about Nic. I confided little details that I hadn't even mentioned to Esther. "These dreams are trying to tell me something. They're trying to tell me to stay away from Nic."

"You think so?" Jessie said incredulously. Her little face wrinkled into a grin. "Sweetie, did you forget our discussion about dreams? This foresight that you have is an amazing gift, but I think it's foolish to let it rule your life. You see pieces, fragments, of the future. You don't know what comes before or after each one. Do your best to be prepared, but don't let these dreams keep you from things that will make you happy."

I opened my mouth to protest, but she put her hand up to stop me.

"Now. You don't have to listen to me; you can do what you like. But I think that Nic should know. Then, once he understands, let him make his own decision. If he thinks it's worth the risk, who are you to try and stop him?" She patted my cheek tenderly and left me, disappearing into her kitchen.

Wandering back to my room I thought back to the night I talked to Jessie. Had I really forgotten her advice? Not all of my dreams had come to fruition in the exact way I had dreamed. Something must have happened to make them different. Maybe if I did tell Nic, together we could change the others.

Now that I had made the decision to tell Nic everything, the day dragged by. I kept going over different conversations in my head, trying to figure out the best way to apologize and explain all that was going on inside of me. I just prayed I wasn't too late and that he would listen.

My rooms were finally finished. I hurried to Nic's dorm.

Out of breath I knocked on the door. "Hey Ben, is Nic here?"

"No, you just missed him. He headed to work," was his reply.

Running back to the restaurant I scoured the room frantically, searching for Nic's tall frame. I spotted him heading to the door to the kitchen.

I hurried across the room hoping to get there before he did.

"Nic," I called out.

He paused when he heard me but didn't turn.

"I need to tell you something," I said.

Nic slowly turned toward me.

"How about this, you can explain tomorrow if you come camping with me."

"Camping? Of course," I agreed as quickly as I could. I would do anything at this point to get him to listen to me.

"Get an extra day off and see if Esther wants to come," he said sounding very businesslike and not like the Nic I knew.

Nic turned and entered the kitchen leaving me standing there staring after him, confused by the conversation. Slowly I turned and left the restaurant.

That night I had another dream.

The just-cut grass was tickling my toes as I ran. I laughed and shrieked, running around bushes and flower beds trying to outrun him, but not really wanting to. I didn't know who he was, but I knew it was his dress shirt I was wearing as I ran. His strong arms that wrapped around my waist and lifted me up into the air when he caught me.

Chapter 14

"Vivian, you need to stay here today. Something terrible might happen to you," Esther said.

"Esther, you can't expect Vivian to stay just because you're too scared to go," Tammy interjected.

I gave Tammy a 'You're not helping' look, took Esther's arm and pulled her back into our room and shut the door.

"What's really going on, sis?" I asked.

"You keep having these dreams and they are creeping me out. What if one comes true and you really get hurt?" she said a little too quietly.

I looked at her and realized that she was really scared that she might lose me too, just like mom.

I put my arms around her and gave her a tight hug.

"I want to go and you should too. It will be fun and it would be good to get away from here for a few days. We will be okay."

"I don't really want to go if Ben is there. He's been avoiding me," Esther said.

"He's not avoiding you. I saw him yesterday after dinner. They have kept him busy because of some issues with the sprinkler lines. He really wants you to come," I said.

I was pleased to see Esther's slow smile and nod.

The day was perfect for our hike. The bright sun was just beginning its travels across a cloudless sky as we pulled our packs out of Nic's jeep. The trail meandered across a wide open field and then disappeared in the pine trees at the other side. It didn't take us long to enter the cool shade of the stately pines. Almost immediately we began the steep ascent to the campsite. I was grateful for the walking sticks Nic had given me. It made climbing the steep trail bearable.

The path leveled out under the shade of aspens.

"Let's stop here and rest," Esther said. "I don't think I can go much further."

"Sounds good," I said as I lowered myself onto a nearby log and slowly slid out of my pack.

Nic strolled over and handed me a water bottle.

"Thanks," I said taking a long drink.

"Hey, do you guys see that?" Ben asked pointing across the ravine.

Nic turned and looked towards the ravine.

"It looks like a mountain lion," he said.

"A lion! Where?" I exclaimed jumping up from my seat on the log.

"Just there," Nic said, putting his arm around me showing me where to look. I saw a large, light brown cat disappear into the trees.

"Esther where are you going?" I heard Ben ask.

"Just out of this mountain and away from that cat."

I turned to see Ben hurry to catch up with her and whisper something in her ear. Esther nodded and came back with Ben's arm around her shoulders.

"I think we are far enough away and we'll be going in the opposite direction," Nic said. "I don't think we have anything to worry about."

The trail narrowed as we climbed higher into the trees. The sun moved further across the sky. Sweat ran down my back under my pack and my legs were beginning to burn. I hoped it wouldn't be much further.

"What do you all think of this space to camp?" Nic called from further up the trail. He had found a flat grassy spot under a canopy of pine and aspen trees. I dropped my pack in a patch of tall grass, stretched and began to unpack. It didn't take long to get the two tents set up and a small fire started in the area we had cleaned out.

"Come on a walk," Nic said.

"Just let me get something out of my pack." I went to where my pack was and pulled out a spiral bound notebook. Nic shoved his hands in his pockets and we wandered off towards the sound of gurgling water.

"I know what you must think of me. But I can explain everything, if you still want me to."

"Okay."

We sat at the edge of a stream on a wide, smooth rock. I handed Nic my dream notebook and waited patiently as he read through the entries skipping to the ones I had marked. Seeing him on horseback, my dream of the dead man on the floor, visions of being stuck cleaning bathrooms just to make ends meet. "And then there was a dream about a fire...you tried to save me, and you didn't make it," I said.

"What do you mean I didn't make it? What happened?"

"We were running, trying to outrun the fire, and you lifted me up. You got me to safety, somehow, but before you could get out, a burning tree landed on top of you." My cheeks flushed, and I could nearly feel the heat of the flames licking at them.

I looked at Nic and watched as he turned and set the notebook on the rock behind him. Shifting back around he took my face gently in his hands. I felt myself slowly sway towards him. I looked into deep pools of blue in his eyes as he lowered his head. My eyelids closed as I felt his lips press to mine. Sliding his hands down my neck, he wrapped his arms around me and pulled me close. His body was warm and strong; exactly what I needed, and what I had been missing all summer.

"Vivian," he said softly against my lips, "Why didn't you tell me? Leaning back slightly he continued. "You've been holding this in all summer? I don't know what's going to happen in the future. But I do know that I want as many moments with you as I can get. We can worry about the future when it comes, just let me be with you." He pulled me even closer until my head was resting against his chest, my arms sliding around his back holding him tight. His heartbeat filled me as I relaxed against him and let myself be swallowed up in this most perfect of moments.

Later after dinner Nic, Ben, Esther, and I circled the fire as the sun finally slipped down behind the mountaintop. One by one, I could see little twinkles of starlight appear in the darkening sky. Nic sat next to me on a log, kept close by the blanket wrapped around our shoulders.

"That was a great hike," Ben said. "We must have come five miles at least."

"At least," I agreed.

"But the way my legs hurt, I wouldn't be surprised if it were ten." Esther nodded emphatically, rubbing her calves. "I don't think I'm going to be able to walk tomorrow," she said. "You might have to carry me back down the mountain." She smiled playfully at Ben.

"It would be my pleasure," he replied. I smiled. It was strange for me to watch my sweet little sister flirting so shamelessly, but I supposed that it was going to happen sooner or later. At least Ben was a nice guy.

"That mountain lion was pretty cool," he continued.

"You mean terrifying?" Esther argued. "I'm amazed we didn't get eaten."

"That was pretty scary," I said quietly to Nic. "I was worried for a while there." It had been startling to see the lion earlier that day, standing proudly on the far hillside, just staring at us.

"Well, just stick with me and there's nothing to worry about," he said, and kissed my forehead. I smiled and leaned into him, but couldn't help noticing him scanning the rocks above us.

"I'm gonna go to bed," Esther yawned. "I can barely keep my eyes open." It was probably only ten, but I understood how she felt. The only thing that kept me from joining her in our tent was Nic's warmth. Esther said goodnight and went to the tent. A few minutes later, Ben left too, zipping up in the tent that he and Nic would be sharing.

"When did you start having dreams like that?" Nic asked suddenly.

"Ummm...I don't know. As long as I can remember, I guess."

"Do they always come true?"

"Not always, but a lot of the time. Even silly things like seeing you on the horse or Esther dumping Mom's perfume down the sink when she was little."

"Really? Even stuff like that?" Nic laughed a little, forming shallow lines around his mouth and eyes. "Wow. Nothing like that has ever happened to me."

"I'm sure you've had déjà vu or something." I pointed out, trying to make my "gift," as Jessie called it, seem less exceptional.

"Well, yeah, but déjà vu is nothing like seeing the future." Nic sighed and lifted his face to the sky. "No, I'm just an ordinary guy. I mean, my life has been pretty good so far, but nothing extraordinary."

"I'm sure that's not true," I said, resting my hand on top of his. "I think you're pretty extraordinary."

He laughed again. "Well, I think you might be a bit biased. But I grew up in your average middle-class American home, average school, average everything. I wonder what it would be like to have a gift like yours—something above average, you know?" He looked at me tenderly, as if having me next to him was as close as he would get.

"Be careful what you wish for," I joked, but as I looked at him I knew that there was something amazing about him under the surface, something unlike anyone else.

After we said goodnight, I laid in my sleeping bag, my eyes wide open. I had been terrified to let Nic in, but now that I had, it felt like an elephant had lifted itself off my chest and I could finally breathe again. The last few weeks I had been floundering, walking around like a shadow. But Nic's smile and the touch of his hand had brought me back to life.

The sounds of the night became nature's lullaby as I lay there snuggled in my sleeping bag. I wonder what Nic was thinking about or if he was already asleep. He had been so wonderful when I told him about my dreams, glad that I finally had the courage to tell him. I felt safe in a way, knowing that he was aware of my dreams and what they could mean. I closed my eyes picturing Nic in his tent, hands folded behind his head. Up there in the mountains, I drifted off to sleep and had the most restful night since the summer began.

Chapter 15

The sky was just beginning to brighten when I crawled out of my tent the next morning. I did my best to be quiet as I got dressed, trying not to wake Esther. She stirred a little when I tripped over the edge of the tent, but eventually I managed to make it out without disturbing her too much.

I wasn't too surprised to find Nic already sitting by the fire pit, stirring the coals with a long stick.

"Hey!" he said, straightening up.

"Hey," I answered. "You're up early."

"Yeah, I thought I would head up the trail a little farther. See if I can make it to the top before we have to head back." He tossed the stick into the small fire. "You want to come with me?"

"Sure. It would be a shame to come this far and not go all the way up." I stuffed the granola bars that Nic handed me into my pack and filled my canteen with water.

"Do you think we should invite Esther?" he asked. "I know Ben would rather sleep in, but she might want to come."

I laughed under my breath. "No, I'll just let her sleep. After yesterday it'll be a miracle if Ben doesn't end up carrying her back down the mountain."

"I'm glad Ben was able to come. I still don't understand why he didn't at least try to see her the past few weeks. They seem to get along really well." I said.

"He's been busy and he's a little worried about the age difference," Nic said. "I know he doesn't want to get to close and hurt her. He's still trying to sort it all out."

I gave an understanding nod and picked up my pack.

It only took about an hour to reach the top, so we curved around to the west side, where the largest peak was. We made it just as the sun did, and together we sat on a boulder and watched it climb higher in the sky. It colored the wispy clouds orange and yellow, and slowly replaced the inkiness of the night sky with a soft cotton candy blue.

"I had a dream last night," Nic said.

"Oh yeah?" I replied, my interest piqued.

"Yeah. About a mountain lion, a really big black one. It was really close to me. I wasn't scared of it," he paused. "But it was really...intense. It just stood there, staring at me with those huge eyes." He took a deep breath of the morning air and smiled. "Probably just because that mountain lion was following us yesterday."

"I don't know," I said. "Jessie says all dreams mean something, not just dreams like mine. She told me about this Native American woman she knows—I think her name is Ella—who taught her all about dreams."

"That Miss Jessie seems to know everything, doesn't she?" Nic laughed.

"You know, I think she might."

Retrieving our cameras from their cases we wandered around the summit. The way the sun hit the rocks, casting lines of shadow in contrasting patterns on its craggy surface, inspired some amazing photos. I found my camera focused in on tender shoots of grass, vibrant green against a field of snowy white. I caught Nic's muscles tighten as he ran his fingers through his light brown hair, causing some to stand on end and flutter in the early morning breeze.

"I hate to brag, but I think we've just taken some of the best pictures ever," I smiled.

"Wait!" Nic commanded. He held up his camera and snapped a picture of me. "Now we have." I laughed.

By nine o'clock we had gone about as high as we could go—not to the very top, but only rock climbers would have been able to go that high. I stood, arms akimbo, looking out around me. "Three peaks," I said, noting a smaller peak to the south, and another to the north.

"It's really beautiful," Nic said. "Thanks for coming with me. No one ever wants to come all the way up here, so I've never made it this far before." I smiled. "Do you mind if we go a bit farther?" Nic asked.

"Yeah, I'm good for a bit more," I said as I took a quick drink and followed him along another rocky path. He looked back at me, smiling, clearly pleased that I could keep up with him.

As we rounded the far side of the peak, we reached a little outcropping in the rock. We had surpassed the tree line, and even though it was well into July the snow still lay in large patches on the mountainside. Beneath the crystalline white, little tufts of green grass poked through, asserting itself in the cold.

"We better stop here and take a break before we head back," Nic suggested. I agreed, not quite ready to leave and break the spell. I took off my pack and found a large rock to sit on. At first, the cold of the hard rock shocked me, but soon I found that it brought some relief to my tired muscles.

Nic walked around the clearing, snapping pictures of anything and everything. For a moment he stopped, and looked off down the path.

"Something wrong?" I asked, wondering if he had seen the mountain lion again.

"Not really. There's someone coming up the path. It looks like they're gonna try to climb to the top, but I really don't think it's a good idea to do that alone." Worry creased his forehead.

I turned to look down the path. Sure enough, there was a lone hiker coming closer to us. As they approached, I saw that it was a woman; I couldn't guess her age, she seemed somehow ageless, but she was very beautiful. Her skin was perfectly smooth and her jaw perfectly shaped, as if Michelangelo had sculpted her out of the finest caramel-colored marble. Her long black hair swayed slightly in the breeze, and it almost looked like she was part of the mountain.

"Here," Nic said, looking at the woman. He took a quick drink from his canteen, and offered it to me. "Drink some water. Don't want you passing out on me," he smiled. I rolled my eyes and accepted the canteen. I took a quick drink, but it was almost empty. I handed it back to him after making sure that there were still a few sips left in it for him.

The woman was nearly to us, and I could see a broad beaming smile on her face. "Absolutely gorgeous, isn't it?" she said. There was something warm and familiar about her voice.

"Yes, it is," I answered, smiling back at her.

"And it's nice to run in to some other hikers," she added. "Would you happen to have some water you could spare?" I noticed that she had no pack—in fact, she had nothing but a richly-colored walking staff covered in intricate carvings. I reached for my canteen, but Nic was quicker.

"You can have this," he said as she took it from his hand. "We don't have a lot. I hope it helps."

The woman stood drinking from the canteen for several seconds. When she finished, it seemed that she was satisfied, but I could have sworn there was only a sip or two left in it. I realized that I must have misjudged the weight of Nic's canteen.

"I'm Ashira," she said, giving Nic his canteen. She took his hand in a firm handshake, and then mine. "What brings you so far up the mountain?"

"Just admiring the view," I explained. "It's a beautiful morning."

"Yes it is." she looked up at the highest peak with a peaceful expression on her pristine face. "There's an undeniable feeling up here. Magical, even spiritual." She closed her eyes and took a deep breath.

"What about you?" Nic asked curiously.

"Oh, I come up here all the time. It's like home to me," she answered. I wondered if she ever did anything but smile.

"Is it safe to climb up by yourself?" I asked, saying what Nic was thinking, "especially when you don't have any gear."

"It's safe, I promise." Ashira's eyes took on an amuse twinkle. "I've got everything I need." She tapped her walking stick on the ground, a leather strap woven with feathers and beads tied around the top.

Nic smiled at her and held out his camera. "Would you take our picture?" he asked.

"Of course!" Ashira agreed, talking the camera from him. Nic put his arms around me and pressed me against him. I hadn't noticed how cold it was this high up, but in his warmth I realized that I had been shivering. Ashira crouched down and, with her walking stick lain across her knees, took a picture of our embrace with the imposing peak rising up behind us.

She moved deftly, taking pictures from several different angles so we would have our pick. Finally, she stood up and gave Nic the camera.

"Thanks, Ashira," Nic said.

"Thank you," she replied. "Enjoy the rest of your hike." She smiled again, and with a wave headed across a wide expanse of snow.

"She must really love it up here," Nic said as he watched her meander off the snow and onto more rocky ground. She looked completely at peace, with herself and with the mountain. "I just hope she doesn't get the idea to camp up here. At this altitude, it's way too cold."

"I'm sure she knows what she's doing," I said. I was impressed by his concern and care, even for a complete stranger; it was one of the qualities that most attracted me to him.

"These are going to be great pictures," he said excitedly, turning his attention back to me.

We set down our packs and got out some granola bars. My stomach was rumbling, and I was looking forward to a big meal when we got back to the resort. I could only imagine what Jessie would have waiting for us when we got back, but a granola bar would have to do for now. As I sat there, looking out at the snowy expanse, I noticed something strange.

"There's something wrong with this picture," I said, more to myself than anything. But Nic heard and raised an eyebrow.

"What?"

"I'm not sure..." I stood and, leaving my pack on the ground, walked across the path to a large snow field on the other side. The farther I walked, the higher the snow got, covering up the tops of my hiking boots. Nic walked along by my side.

"Wait here for a second," I said. Taking about ten more steps, I turned around and came back. "Do you see that?" I asked.

"What do you mean? Your tracks in the snow?"

"Yes. My tracks, but just mine," I explained. "Ashira left this way, right over this field, but there aren't any tracks other than mine."

"You're right!" Nic said. "This seems beyond weird." He stared at the snow, no doubt puzzling over how it was possible.

A large bird circled overhead. I didn't know enough about birds to name it, but I could guess that it was rare, and I certainly knew it was beautiful.

"Well, we should head back. We'll have to pack up and get going soon."

"Okay," Nic agreed. "But just one more picture, okay?"

I shook my head amusedly. "Fine, but it had better be a good one." We gathered up our packs and approached a log that he had chosen for the shot. "How do you want me?"

"Surprise me," he said with a smile. He turned away, his camera already poised by his eye, and counted down as he took a few steps. I planted my hands on the log and looked up to the sky, just as I had last summer by the lake. "Five..." he said, "Four...Three...Two...One!" He pivoted around, but instead of taking the picture, he stopped, and lowered the camera slowly. His face was expressionless, statuesque.

"What? You don't like this pose?" I asked, suddenly self-conscious. I started to move my legs, but he stopped me.

"Don't move," he said softly. Noiselessly, he came toward me, putting the camera in my hand. Firmly taking the other, he pulled me off the log. "Do not turn around. Just keep walking, slowly."

"What is it—"I tried to turn around, but his grip was too strong.

"Just keep walking," I did as I was told, becoming puzzled and a bit frightened. There was an intensity in his eyes that alarmed me.

"Will you at least let me take your picture?" I asked.

Despite his warnings, I turned around, frozen. Poised not five feet from where I had been sitting was a dark brown cat. A wide, black streak fell from its forehead to the end of its nose. Its large paws spread on the rock beneath. It stared at us with liquid gold eyes.

The breeze slowly stilled and the birds went silent. For an eternity, none of us moved. Without thinking I slowly raised Nic's camera and tapped the shutter button. I didn't realize how risky that had been until I heard the click of the shutter. My muscles tightened, waiting for the lion to pounce. The cat didn't move.

As if broken from a spell, Nic began to walk backward almost as if in slow motion, his hand reaching out, searching for mine.

Our fingers brushed and Nic grasped mine firmly. We backed slowly away, our eyes never leaving the massive animal. It vaulted off the rock and bounded away.

I wasn't sure if either of us drew breath until the lion was out of sight.

Nic took another deep breath, turned, and wrapped me in a tight, almost crushing hug.

"You took a picture?" he said incredulously. "A mountain lion looking right at us, and you thought it was a good idea to take a picture?"

I laughed and hugged him back. "Yeah, I guess I did."

"You're incredible," he let go and adjusted his pack. "I can't wait to get that one developed."

Running back up the trail I retrieved my pack and we started back to camp.

We told Ben and Esther about our adventure, but despite their "oohs" and "ahhs," I wasn't sure they believed us. That was okay, I decided. It would be another memory, another moment that would stay just between Nic and I.

The lights on the vast stage were almost blinding. The room was almost completely dark but I could see that every seat was occupied. Standing next to me was a tall, broad shouldered man in an expensive suit. He stood there seemingly casually but I could sense the excitement tensing his muscles. He spoke with such confidence. I knew deep inside that I was standing by Nic.

He looked over at me with an adoring glance. I knew I belonged on the stage, feeling elegant in an emerald green pencil skirt with matching short jacket. Without hesitating, I began to speak. I felt at ease in this place, like this wasn't the first time.

Chapter 16

"I guess you and Ben worked everything out. Are you dating now?" I asked Esther as we headed to the river to meet the girls.

"He saw me walking home from work the other day and we wandered around for an hour just talking," Esther said. "He was worried about our ages, can you believe it?" I could hear the shock in her voice.

"Well, you are still 18," I said.

"Only for a few more months," she retorted.

"So, what did you do?" I questioned, not wanting to start an argument. "You looked all dressed up when you came home tonight."

"We went into town to the new restaurant we've been hearing about. It wasn't your usual 'steak and potato' place you see so much up here," she said. "It was a high end Italian place."

I could see a dreamy look fill her eyes.

"Well don't keep me in suspense. What did you do after the obviously romantic dinner?"

"He took me to a foreign film. It was crazy having to read the subtitles the whole time. Ben kept whispering the romantic scenes in my ear. It was so exaggerated I had to bite my lip to keep from laughing. He is such a comedian," Esther said with a silly grin on her face.

Quiet laughter tumbled over us as we went around the bend in the path. I noticed Esther began to fiddle nervously with the yellow towel draped over her shoulder.

"What took you two so long to get here? Rochelle even beat you and you all know how she just loves our skinny dippin' tradition," Kenny said as she threw a sassy grin towards Rochelle who was sunk deep in the water.

I quickly undressed and slid in. Looking around I found Esther slowly undressing in the shadows. I knew she was a little uncertain about coming tonight. Not wanting to draw attention to her I turned to Rochelle.

"What did you end up doing last night? I thought you were going to work on your painting?"

"I did for a while but my back started hurting so I came down here to soak for a while," she said.

Glancing at Esther as she slid in the water beside me, I gave her a quick smile and turned back to Rochelle.

"I was hoping to have the place to myself but when I got here, there was this guy already in the water. He was a guest. I've seen him around a couple of times this week," Rochelle continued.

"Uh oh," I said. We all smiled, sure we knew what was coming next.

"Well, I was just going to ignore him, but he kept looking at me and smiling while I dressed down to my swimsuit. That was a bit awkward."

I could see her blush and could tell this was a little awkward for her as well, but I was glad when she returned to her story.

"Anyway, I was putting my clothes on the rock and I kind of slipped and my flip flops went flying into the water."

"Come on, Rochelle, where's the good stuff?" Kenny interrupted jokingly, "If this was Kimi's story you'd be making out already."

Kimi took a little bow in the inky water, obviously proud of the reputation she'd established.

"Hold on, hold on," Rochelle admonished. "So, I was gonna go in and get them, but he reached down and grabbed them before I had a chance. Then, when he gave them back he started talking to me. We talked for almost 2 hours!"

"And?" Kimi asked impatiently.

"And...he walked me back to the cabin...and kissed me goodnight." Her face flushed bright red.

"Nice!" Kimi cheered.

"Yeah, nice." Kenny agreed. "But you know if a manager finds out, you're toast."

"I know," Rochelle admitted. "But he was so handsome and easy to talk to. I mean, he's got to be 6'4", and he's got the sexiest brown eyes."

"And he was shirtless," Kenny pointed out.

"Yeah, well that didn't hurt," Rochelle admitted. "But we have so much in common, and he was such a gentleman when he dropped me off. He asked my permission before he kissed me!" she declared. All of us raised our eyebrows in amazement.

"Looks like you found your prince charming," Tammy sighed. "While the rest of us are still kissing frogs."

"As long as the frogs are good at kissing, I don't mind," Kimi countered. We all laughed and I thought of Nic.

"I don't know..." Kenny said. "Vivian has been pretty smiley the last couple of days. Anything you haven't told us?" she eyed me suspiciously.

"Well," I began, "We talked and hiked and I told Nic everything. He wasn't upset and I think he understood. So, everything is good between us."

"Hallelujah!" Tammy cried. "I've been waiting for this all summer. It has been torture watching you two be miserable, since we all know you belong together."

"So, tell us about this hike," Kenny pressed.

"We almost got eaten by a mountain lion," I said, watching their eyes widen. But as I told the story, I couldn't get that phrase out of my head; belong together. Despite my nightmares, I was beginning to think that maybe we did.

"Vivian! Vivian! Wake up."

I rolled over and through blurry eyes, looked at my clock, 12:57am. Who wanted me awake. It was the middle of the night; at least it felt like it to me.

"Vivian get up," I heard it more clearly this time. It was definitely male.

"Just go answer the door," moaned Esther.

"Fine," I muttered as I climbed out of bed. Dragging a blanket with me I flung it around my shoulders and tried to find my flip flops. Grumbling, I finally found them pushed under my bed. Sliding them on I shuffled to the door and peaked out.

"Nic, what are you doing here?" I whispered.

Reaching out Nic grabbed the blanket and pulled me out into the hall.

"I couldn't sleep," he said. "Come walk with me."

Even as I looked at him like he was out of his mind, I heard myself say. "Ok."

He took my hand and we headed out into the night.

We started wandering up and down the dark, quiet road.

"What's going on, Nic?" I asked as I stopped and turned to face him. "I don't think you woke me up in the middle of the night just to walk around a dusty road."

"No, I didn't. I can't sleep. I just can't get you out of my head." Placing his hands on my shoulders he pulled me closer. "What are you doing to me Vivian Lewis?" he whispered just before his mouth crushed mine in a deep urgent melding of mouths.

I could feel the ripple of muscles hardened beneath my hands as I slid my arms around his back and held him close. His breath caressed my lips.

"Viv?"

"Ya?" I said, wishing he would kiss me again.

"Would you be my girl?"

Pushing up on my toes, I whispered, "Yes" before pressing my lips to his.

Chapter 17

I was so glad I explained everything to Nic. The past few weeks were wonderful. I felt bad about all the time we missed being together.

"Vivian?" Nic asked.

"What do you think about going hiking tomorrow? It will probably take all day."

We were standing in line waiting to get our dinner when he made the suggestion.

I took a hoagie sandwich and put it on my plate. Turning to Nic, "That sounds like fun to me," I said.

Reaching for two bags of chips I put one on my tray and handed the other to Nic.

"Who's all coming?" I asked.

"Not sure. Ben is the one planning it. He heard about some different hikes from a guest. It's about an hour drive north of here, but he said there's one in an amazing canyon and follows a river the whole way."

That sounded fun to me. We had pretty much stayed around the resort for the past couple of weeks. It would be nice to get away. I was already looking forward to spending the entire day with Nic.

The next morning found the nine of us piling into Nic's jeep and Kyle's car. Alex changed his mind because his girlfriend called and was surprising him with a visit that day.

"Where's Esther?" Nic asked as we drove out onto the highway.

"She changed her mind last night. She just wants to hang out at the pool and read. She also said she didn't dare go anywhere with me because she was afraid my 'weird', her word not mine, dreams would come true. I don't know if they will or not but I can't live my life always afraid," I said.

"Ben's going to be bummed," Nic said with a laugh.

He smiled at me and went back to driving. A little less than an hour later, we turned off at a trail head. After parking, we retrieved our daypacks and headed off down the trail. There was a lot of flirting and laughter as we walked. It wasn't a very difficult hike and we returned to our cars quicker than expected.

"That was a short hike," Kenny said. "I was expecting something a little more intense."

"That was fine with me," I said. "I got some great pictures."

"Oh, is that what you and Nic were doing back there," Kimi teased, "taking pictures?"

We found a shady picnic area a few miles down the road and stopped to enjoy the lunch Jessie had prepared for us. It wasn't long, though before we became antsy to be off on another adventure. Hidden waterfalls, wide open meadows, and fields of bison, were a few of the treasures we came across as we continued our hike.

Large fluffy clouds were forming around the high peaks as we made our way around the small lake at the base of the mountain and back to the jeep. The afternoon sun had beat down, causing my shirt to stick to my moist back. I was glad to be back in the air-conditioned jeep.

We had only been driving about 20 minutes when Nic pulled his jeep onto a scenic byway. I looked up and saw Kyle's car pull over into a nearby parking area.

"Tammy wants to go on one more hike before we head back; do you mind?" Kyle asked as we climbed out of the jeep. Everyone seemed good with it.

The hike was about a mile, beginning at this parking area and ending at another parking area to the south of us. It dropped down into a gorgeous canyon with a beautiful, clear flowing river that snaked through the bottom.

"I think this is the trail we were looking for earlier," said Ben excitedly.

The sun was high in the western sky and the air was still hot. We all started off down the gravel path.

It was great. Nic and I took our time, enjoying the view, taking pictures and just being together. Flowers, dried from the hot August sun were scattered around rocks and in the grass. It hadn't rained much that summer and everything was drying up, except on the far side of the river. The rock cliffs rose almost straight up out of the water. The cracks in the rocks were home to small purple blooms as well as large red blossoms which stood out against the moist gray of the rock wall. The proximity to the river gave them enough moisture to remain in bloom this late in the year.

"I wish we could get across there," I said pointing to the far side, as we continued to follow the path.

"Me, too," said Nic trying to get a close up of a cluster of red blossoms protruding from the rocks some 30 yards away.

We continued to follow the path beside the river, not in any hurry. When we were a little more than halfway to the upper parking area at the end of the trail, we came to a wide spot in the river. It was off the trail and down a steep grass covered hill. The river moved slowly there, and a small beach area below us was the perfect place to take a swim. Tammy and Kimi were the first to spread out their towels close to the river. Tony dropped his pack, toed off his shoes and plowed into the water, intentionally splashing the girls.

"Hey!" yelled Tammy grabbing her once dry towel. Kimi ran to the water's edge and began splashing him back. Soon Kyle and Rochelle joined in. We watched our friends ahead of us, joking and laughing.

"It's probably a good thing you're holding that camera," said Nic.

I didn't know what he meant by that.

"Why? Do you want me to take their picture?"

"Yeah," he said with a smile.

I turned back to the river and started taking pictures of our friends in the water. I didn't notice Nic take off his pack and put his camera in it.

"Let me take your pack for you." What a gentleman I thought, taking it off and handing it to him. He held it for a moment while I focused in on a few more shots.

"How does it look?" he asked putting out his hand for my camera.

Not thinking about it, I just handed him my camera. Instead of looking through the lens, he gently put the cover on, and placed the camera carefully in my pack.

Before I knew what was happening, Nic had my hand and I was off my feet and over his shoulder.

He ran yelling towards the river. "Nic!" I shrieked as we both hit the cold water. It wasn't very deep and we came up laughing. Our friends joined in and soon we were in the middle of a colossal water fight.

I had my clothes on over my swimsuit. Sloshing out of the river I peeled them off and found a patch of grass to lay them to dry in the sun.

A very wet shirt landed on my back. Nic just grinned as I recognized his shirt lying on the grass. I shook it out and laid it next to mine, then ran back to join Nic. Since the river was so wide at this point, we could swim across without the current pushing us down stream too much. We swam to the far side where the flowers were. Holding on to the rock cliff, I reached out to touch one of the soft petals. Treading water Nic slid an arm around me and pulled me close.

"Are you having fun?" he asked after a minute to catch our breath.

"Yeah. I am," I said admiring the view in this beautiful narrow canyon.

The swirling of water was mesmerizing, tiny whirlpools slowly moved around rocks as they made their way downstream. The laughter of our friends faded from my attention as I gazed into Nic's blue eyes. I placed my arms around his neck and pulled myself close, feeling the muscles of his chest against me. I laid my head on his shoulder.

After a moment, Nic broke the silence, "What are you thinking?" he asked.

"I was just thinking how beautiful this place is and..."

"And what?" asked Nic puzzled.

"And some dork got my clothes wet!" I said as I pushed off the rocks, splashed Nic in the face and swam frantically across the river with him right behind me.

I made it halfway when he caught me. We were both laughing so hard it was difficult to breathe. He pulled me to the shore and before I could get my composure, hugged me close. His lips hovered a breath above mine. I glanced up into his face just before my eyes closed. His lips gently caressed mine before pressing harder. My arms slid around his back pulling him close.

"Wooo!" yelled Kimi.

Nic looked down at my blushing face and grinned. A shiver ran up my spine as I backed out of his arms, gave him a smile and ran out of the river. With my towel spread out on the sand, I laid back and closed my eyes; enjoying the heat of the sun as it dried my cool, skin.

"Mind if I join you?" Nic had retrieved his pack as well and had his towel over his tan shoulders.

I smiled at him as he lay down beside me. Neither of us spoke. After a few minutes, Nic moved his hand over, his fingers mingling with mine.

"Hey you lovebirds," interrupted Kyle as he came walking down the path towards them. "Unless we all want to take the long way and hike back, a couple of us need to go get the cars and drive them to the upper side of the trailhead," he said, looking at Nic.

Nic got up, taking his towel, shirt, and pack "Back in a minute," he said with a wink.

I watched as he and Kyle headed off down the trail. Closing my eyes, I drifted off as my mind wandered back to all that had happened this summer. The trail ride, skinny dipping, the woman on the mountain and now all the laughter and flirting of today.

Chapter 18

"Hey, Viv. Where are the other guys?" I opened my eyes. The high cliff to our west was now casting a shadow on our swimming hole and a slight breeze made me a little chilly. I sat up, pulling my towel around me.

"They went back to take the cars to the upper end of the trail. I think it's closer. We won't have to hike so far."

Rochelle came and sat down beside me. "So, you and Nic..." she said, teasing.

I shrugged my shoulders, but couldn't hide my smile. We both started to laugh.

Our laughter died off and we just sat there, musing about the scene before us; the slow moving water, our friends, the puffy white and grey clouds in the sky, the gentle breeze.

"Look at those trees up there," said Rochelle casually. On top of the cliffs high above us, the large pines swayed heavily in the wind.

"Wow. It must be blowing pretty hard up there," I said not thinking much of it. "Barely a breeze down here."

"Hey, ladies," said Ben, coming up and shaking his head. The water from his hair sprinkled down on us.

"Ben!" said Rochelle, annoyed at his playfulness.

He sat down beside us. "Anyone hungry? I smell barbeque."

I was getting kind of hungry. I took a big deep breath in through my nose. "Yeah barbe..." I started to say, then stopped. Wait, I thought. I took in another breath, looking at Ben, who was still smiling. He slowly turned, his smile fading.

"That's not a barbeque," said Rochelle looking up. The high fluffy white clouds that we had seen earlier coming from the west were now obscured by lower, fast moving smoke blowing in from the east.

I looked at Rochelle, who swallowed hard, then at Ben. We had seen the sign for the campsites to the east of us. It was probably just a little campfire, I told myself. "I think we need to get going," I said, trying to remain calm.

"Yeah. I think you're right," said Ben.

Rochelle and I gathered our things as Ben walked quickly to get his pack, constantly looking back to the east.

I wish Nic would hurry back, I thought, looking up the hill to the trail but seeing no one. A weird feeling came over me. "Guys," I said loud enough to get their attention. "It's getting late. We need to get going."

Ben had retrieved his day pack and hurried back to Rochelle and I.

"Let's go meet Nic and Kyle so they don't have to hike so far back," I said quietly.

"Okay," nodded Ben but he wasn't looking at me. He was still looking at the thickening smoke.

"Do you smell that?" asked Tammy wandering over.

"It's bacon," yelled Tony.

"Yummy!" laughed Kimi.

"Seriously guys. We need to go," said Ben loud enough for those by the river to hear.

"Shouldn't we wait for Kyle and Nic?" asked Tammy as she slowly gathered her things.

"We'll meet them halfway," said Ben.

I looked over to see Kenny wading in the shallow water, tossing rocks into the current. She seemed so distracted.

"Kenny, we need to get out of here," I yelled.

"Okay,"

I threw my pack over my shoulder and followed Ben and Rochelle up the hill. At the top my body froze, my eyes fixed on the billowing smoke coming from behind the trees.

"Everyone up here. Now!" Ben yelled.

"Stay here," he said. I nodded as he dropped his pack and half ran, half slid down the hill to the others.

I turned back to see the smoke getting worse. Strong gusts of wind were blowing towards us. Panic spread through me like molasses, then liquefied when I saw the flames. They licked the trees with their fiery tongues as they advanced.

I closed my eyes tightly; this can't be happening! It's just another dream.

Deep, burning coughs attacked my lungs as the smoke carrying the stench of burning vegetation swirled, propelled me back to reality. Rochelle was standing beside me saying nothing; I could see the fear blatant in her face.

"We've gotta get out of here now," I shouted, looking wildly around for Ben. I could see him down with Kenny haphazardly throwing items in her bag.

Tammy, Kimi, and Tony stumble to a standstill at my side.

"What's going o...?" Kimi said. "Fire," the word fell in a whisper from her lips.

I searched the trail; the smoke obscured my view, still no Nic.

"Let's get back to the cars," said Tammy moving back down the path.

Rochelle reached out, "The guys are this way," she said, directing Tammy up the incline.

The ever increasing popping and crackling of the fire fanned the flames of fear inside me.

"Come on you guys, let's get to the cars!" I screamed.

I plunged into the ever thickening smoke pulling Kimi with me. Through the eerie discord I heard Ben, trusting he had Kenny and Tony, I pressed forward. I kept my head down, my burning eyes on the trail.

I knew the road was about a hundred yards to our east but could see that the flames had already jumped it and were heading straight for us. I coughed again looking down the hill. Kenny was halfway up with Benjamin pushing her from behind. When they finally reached the trail, Kenny froze in panic beside Tony and Kimi who were still not moving, just staring at the oncoming flames.

"Vivian!" yelled Ben, "Get going," he gestured up the trail.

I started back up the trail, making sure the others were following. Ben pushed Kimi and Kenny, plowing them forward. I could see Tony not moving behind Ben.

"Tony! Come on," I yelled.

Ben turned and saw Tony. Running back, Ben grabbed his arm and began to drag him up the trail. Tony started to run, heading toward me. We all began to sprint down the trail. Ben was bringing up the rear making sure everyone was moving.

The smoke was getting worse. I was coughing and choking from it, and the running made it worse. I thought the parking area couldn't be too far away. After running about 50 yards, I slowed to look back. Rochelle was right behind me. The others were spaced out and I could barely see Ben at the very back.

I knew I had to help the others get out. For some reason I felt it was my responsibility. They were slowing down and starting to panic. I could hear Kenny crying.

I squinted and tried to make my way through the increasing smoke.

At the top of a rise in the trail, I could feel the full force of the wind gusts and the heat of the flames approaching less than 30 yards from us.

I can't do this by myself, I thought.

The wind slowed to a standstill. The muted voices of my friends were a broken tape player struggling to get the words out. My face was cooking in the heat of the flames.

"Help," I said. It came out as a whisper. I felt like I was going to pass out. The smoke was too much.

"Vivian!" I heard a man's voice. It was Nic. My eyes were still partly closed when, through the smoke a powerful yet gentle hand grabbed mine. I stumbled as he pulled me to the side of the trail.

"Everyone to the river!" he yelled. The six behind us followed frantically. As we slid down the hill to the water's edge, I could hardly open my eyes. They were stinging so badly from the smoke.

My vision was blurred, but I could see Nic on my left side and others on my right. The smoke was more above and behind us as the wind blew the flames closer to the trail we were just on.

"What do we do?" a girl's voice came from behind us.

Across the river was the sheer cliff rising high above us. The canyon narrowed creating a large waterfall thirty yards downstream. A smaller waterfall fell into a pool in front of us.

"Are we just going to stand here?" Tammy screamed. At that moment a large burning tree fell behind us. The flames were coming quickly, devouring the dry grass that came down, almost to the water's edge.

"Nope!" Nic shouted. He looked at me. I could now see his face clearly. I could tell he was scared, but not panicking. He looked up for a moment then back at me. A look of resolute determination on his face.

"Do you trust me?"

I nodded.

"Come on!" He plunged into the river heading up stream toward the falls, towing me behind him. The cold water no longer rejuvenated but triggered a perilous feeling of foreboding.

The others were staring at the blaze as it incinerated the dry grass on its way to the river. Frantically they rushed into the water after us.

Nic had reached the falls, but was neck deep in water and the falls was nearly seven feet above his head and were three or four feet wide. As I worked my way over to him, he moved to the side of the falls and began to climb up the rocks.

"Vivian, get Ben to me," Nic yelled.

"Ben!" I yelled. In frenzied desperation I waved my arms hoping to catch Ben's attention.

Seeing me he swam against the current to get to me passing the others. We both turned to look up at Nic. "Get up here!" he barked at Ben.

Ben scrambled out of the water and up the slippery rocks.

"Get up there!" yelled Nic.

"No! Girls first," Ben yelled over the sound of the rushing water on one side and the approaching flames on the other.

"Move your ass! You're going to pull us up," ordered Nic as he grabbed the back of Ben's belt and heaved him up. Ben understood and reached for the rocks above him trying to get a hand hold. Even though Ben was heavier, Nic pushed his feet almost throwing his friend over the top. Once there, Nic turned to me and put his hand out.

"Come on!"

I started towards him, then paused and turned. The others were trying to get to us, Kimi, Tammy, Rochelle, Kenny, and Tony.

Without stopping to think I swam back, captured Kimi who was staring blindly into the furnace behind us and pulled her through the water to Nic. The other girls were right behind me now. Kenny was next, then Rochelle. Tammy looked at me as Rochelle climbed the slick rocks next to Nic. I gave her a quick hug then pushed her up towards Nic.

Tony didn't move when it was his turn. He stood in the chest deep water, hypnotized by the flames. I swam frantically towards him, yelling his name as I went. Startled out of the fiery spell he was in Tony charged through the water to Nic who gripped the back of his shirt, while I pushed his butt up the rocks. Ben was there waiting to haul him up. I was the last one. I looked up at Nic still perched on the slippery wet rocks above me. His hand banded itself around my arm as he hauled me up to balance on the narrow shelf.

As I looked into his blue eyes, he kissed me, the fire and water faded away. In that moment time ceased to exist.

There are certain experiences in a person's life that change them. Cathartic points that afterwards, your life is never the same. Defining moments of one's existence. I just stared into his eyes and into his soul. It only lasted a microsecond, but felt like an eternity.

The pressure of Nic's hands was almost painful as he reached down and grabbed my thighs and with surprising strength, threw me up over his head into Ben's waiting arms.

Ben was laying on his stomach, half in the water and half on the rocks. I saw the others stumble through the water, making their way to the cars. I turned back realizing they would be okay on the asphalt parking lot.

Ben tried to help me towards the side but I resisted. "Pull him up! Pull him up!" I ordered frantically.

Ben began to turn back to Nic when we heard a deafening crack. An immense burning log had broken loose and was careening down the hillside towards us. I seized Ben's arm and pulled him backwards as hard as I could, landing us on our backs in the cold water.

My fear ricocheted off the canyon wall as the log went airborne and landed in the spot where Ben had been. I sat up, frozen as I watched in slow motion as the still burning log tipped and went over the falls right above Nic.

"Nic!" The scream burst from me.

Chapter 19

I scrambled towards the edge of the falls, searching for Nic.

I watched anxiously as Ben disappeared over the side. Find him, Ben. Please find him, I prayed.

I crawled closer. Stretched out in the water, my arm hung over the falls failing in its search for Nic. The icy water closed around me, numbness seeped in.

"Ben, where are you?" I yelled. "I can't see Nic!"

"We're by the side. Can you come closer?"

I dragged my frozen body over the slippery rocks and found a heavy branch suspended over the water. I wrapped my arm around it and reached out, straining.

Ben came into view, assisting Nic through the swiftly moving water. With Ben's aid, Nic slowly made his way to an outcropping to one side of the falls. My finger brushed his cold hand. Frantic, I grasped it and held on. Bit by bit Nic inched his way up to safety.

My frozen arm was locked around Nic's waist as the three of us stumbled to the bank and made our way to the jeep. Nic's limp becoming more apparent with every step. Ben took Nic's keys and ran ahead.

Tears welled in my eyes as I watched Nic carefully climb in the jeep. I slid in and carefully sat on his lap. Everyone else had piled in the backseat. Thick, choking smoke swirled around as Ben sped out of the parking lot. He didn't slow down, not with the fire closing in.

"Ben, how's Kyle?" Nic asked through deep, labored breaths.

"I don't know man," Ben yelled back. "I'm sure he got out, though."

Nic's eyes started to close. I bent close to him

"Are you ok?"

"Ya," Nic whispered. "Get us to the resort, Ben"

"No man, we're getting you to the hospital."

"I'll be ok, just go to the resort."

The foreboding, flashing lights pushed through the ever thickening clouds of smoke, signaling the arrival of the approaching emergency vehicles.

I calmed a little when we turned onto the main highway. No more sharp curves and Ben pushed the jeep to go even faster. In record time, we were pulling into the parking lot at the resort.

We scrambled out, careful of Nic. His head leaned back against the seat, his eyes closed.

"What now?" Kimi asked hesitantly.

I saw Kennedy reached over and pulled her into a hug. "Everything will be ok. Here comes Jessie."

"Kenny, you get everyone up to the lounge." Jessie yelled as she ran across the parking lot. "There's help there."

Deep coughs could be heard as Kenny and the others hurried off.

I felt Jessie's hand on my shoulder.

"Let's get him to the hospital. That arm needs to be looked at," she said.

I climbed in the company van after Nic. A slender woman with long black hair sat in front. She said her name was Ella, a friend of Jessie's.

Nic groaned, bringing my attention back to him.

"Nic?" I said, putting my hand on his leg. "Nic?" His arm looked swollen beneath the sleeve of his t-shirt.

"Jessie? What do I do?" I cried. "He's hurting."

His pain filled eyes looked at me for a moment before his dark lashes fluttered closed.

"Don't worry, sweetie. Ella will help him," Jessie answered.

Ella climbed into the seat next to Nic and wrapped her hands carefully around his forearm. There was a slight jerk and a sickening pop. The painful noise that escaped Nic and the solitary tear that ran down his cheek wrenched at my already tender heart. Ella kept her hands on Nic's arm and shoulder for the remainder of the worrisome ride to the hospital. The longer she held his arm the more I could see Nic begin to relax. I reached over and wiped the tear. He opened his eyes and gave me a smile, then resting his head against my shoulder he closed his eyes.

The smooth, sliding, glass doors opened to display the noise and chaos of the hospital. A kind volunteer offered us each a blanket and directed us to the crowded waiting room. Leaning against me Nic hobbled deeper into the room and lowered himself into the nearest empty chair.

Chills permeated my body reminding me of the wet clothes sticking to my cold skin. I unfolded one of the blankets and wrapped it snuggly around Nic. I pulled the other one tightly around my shoulders. A delicious warmth spread through me, the soft blanket dispelling the cold that had taken over me.

Nic had grown heavy, leaning against me while we waited his turn. The sound of his relaxed breathing made me wonder how he could fall asleep amid all this noise. Jessie and Ella were a few feet away in a whispered conversation when a nurse came up to escort Nic back to the emergency room. Ella turned and wordlessly followed Nic.

At Nic's request Jessie asked the doctors to check me. Other than being exhausted, wet and covered in soot, I was fine.

The black, plastic chair grew harder the longer I waited. I felt more than saw Jessie sit next to me. The comfort of her arm felt so much like my mother's. Feeling suddenly exhausted I leaned into her hug and let the tears I had been holding back go free. She held me until my tears subsided.

"Do you think they might know if Kyle is here?" I asked Jessie.

"Let's go check," she said.

We walked over to the nurses' station and a kind young nurse directed us to where he was. Jessie pulled back the curtain I was surprised to see Ella sitting there beside a sleeping Kyle.

"How is he?" I said softly.

"The doctors said he will be alright, they just want to keep him overnight for observation because of the smoke in his lungs," she said. Her soft voice drifted around us.

"Are you Vivian?" a nurse asked quietly as she pulled aside the partition. "There's a guy in here who swears he heard a girl named Vivian's voice. She smiled as she held back the curtain. I recognized that half smile instantly.

"How do you feel?" I asked Nic as I hurried towards him.

"I've been better," he said.

"I'm so sorry you were hurt," I said as the tears pooling in my eyes began to fall.

"Come here," said Nic reaching for me with his good arm.

I moved closer to him and he pulled me down to sit by him. He wrapped his arm around me and held me close while I cried.

"None of this was your fault, Vivian," he said.

"But my dream..."

"Your dream probably saved us. I'm glad you decided to tell me," he said.

"So am I," I replied.

The doctor said Nic had two broken toes and a nasty bruise on his hip, but to everyone's' surprise, his wrist and shoulder were merely sprained. I eyed Ella suspiciously as we climbed back into the van, wondering if she had anything to do with that.

We returned to the resort around 2 in the morning. I could scarcely keep my eyes open. Nic walked me to my room. A sob escaped when I saw Esther's tear stained face. One step was all it took to be in each other's arms.

"Try to sleep," Nic said tenderly. I felt a soft kiss on the top of my head. With a quiet click of the door he was gone.

The next afternoon we sat with our friends in the employee lounge. The warmth of Nic's hand cradled mine, his calloused fingers absentmindedly caressed my palm. I snuggled closer, reassured by the solid muscles pressed against my side.

"Tony isn't coming back," Rochelle said as she walked in, sinking onto the couch beside me. "I heard he just packed up last night and went home."

"That's too bad," Alex answered. He sat on the other couch between his girlfriend and Esther.

"I'm not surprised," I said, remembering the blank look on his face, how he stood paralyzed in the water. "He was really shaken up."

"Tammy too," Esther said. "She's already packed so she can leave after her shift."

"Really?" Alex questioned. "But she seemed okay when I saw her."

"Yeah, well she just doesn't think she can stay here anymore, after what has happened. And business has slowed down a lot, with the fires keeping all the tourists away," Esther said.

"It's true—I heard the managers talking a little while ago," Rochelle said. "They're trying to decide if they should close early this year, since the authorities are warning people to stay away. There's no point in staying open the rest of the season if reservations are being cancelled."

Alex's eyes widened and he squeezed his girlfriend's hand. "Close early? But that's a month of work. I really need the money."

"It's not official," Rochelle reassured him, "I just heard them discussing it." Alex did not look comforted. "But Kyle is coming back later today."

Kyle had stayed behind to help a family get their frightened, young children in the beat up old station wagon. He'd jumped in with them and ended up at the hospital.

Rochelle continued, trying to lift the mood. "They wanted to keep him in the hospital for another day, but he wouldn't hear it."

"Well, however it all turns out," Esther said to Alex, "at least you're all okay."

I looked over at Nic, who had drifted off to sleep next to me.

"Yes," I said quietly. I would always remember the sight of him disappearing under the flaming log, but at least now I understood. As Jessie had said, the dream was a caution, trying to keep us all safe. I was glad I had listened to my friends before I let my dreams separate Nic and I for forever.

Chapter 20

Life settled back into somewhat of a routine. The resort was going to close early but not for another three weeks. We still had guests and rooms to take care of. A fair number of employees had left, but Esther and I decided to stay until the end.

"Have you told Nic that you are staying?" Esther asked as we walked to breakfast one sunny morning. It was hard to believe there were still fires burning, when above us was a beautiful clear blue sky. The winds that had howled during the night had blown most of the smoke away.

"No, not yet, I was hoping to catch him before his shift tonight and talk to him."

"Will you be ok when he leaves?" she asked.

"I don't know. I don't like thinking about not seeing him every day," I said. "I am going to miss him so much."

"What's with the gloomy face?" Rochelle asked as she walked up.

"Sorry," I said. "Just thinking about Nic, he's leaving tomorrow."

She swung her arm around my shoulder and gave me a quick hug.

"We'll just have to find plenty to do to keep you busy, then," she said.

I was excited to see Nic waiting in the front of the line for breakfast when we walked in. I hurried over to him, pulling Esther and Rochelle along behind me.

"Hey, handsome, didn't think I would see you up this early," I said as I slid my arms around his waist, "thought you pulled the late shift."

"I was going to sleep in but Ben woke me up. Man, that guy can't be quiet even if his life depended on it," Nic said chuckling to himself. "I figured I was awake so I might as well get up and hobble on over here. I'm glad I was here early enough to see you all," he said talking to the three of us but his eyes never left mine.

"How was work last night?" I asked, probably not too fun with taped up toes."

"I managed, but the ice I put on it after sure felt good."

"Vivian, quit making eyes at Nic and get your breakfast, you're holding up the line," Kenny called from behind us.

"Sorry," I said glancing back at her. Turning back to Nic with a smile, I grabbed our trays.

We found a large, empty table near the far side of the room. Within just a few minutes it had filled up with all our friends.

"So, I hear you and Esther have decided to stay until close," Kennedy said as she pulled out her chair across from me and sat down. I gave her a glare and nodded.

Nic turned and looked at me, the surprise evident on his face.

"Nic, Esther and I talked about it last night and decided to stay. I was going to tell you tonight after work," I said.

"I have to be to work early so you would have missed me," Nic responded. "How about you meet me after my shift at 9:00 and we'll talk?"

"That sounds good," I said as I tried to wink. Nic smiled.

We dug into our breakfast, hot toasty waffles covered in strawberries with tall, ice cold glasses of orange juice.

"Girls, we better get out of here if we are going to get to work on time," Rochelle said as she picked up her tray and stood up.

I leaned over and gave Nic a quick kiss on the cheek. "See you tonight," I said as I got up to go.

"Hey dad, Esther and I wanted to call and let you know we are staying a few more weeks," I said.

We sat on our pillows in the hall, our heads resting against each other holding the phone suspended between us.

"I'm glad you two called, there is something I wanted to tell you and didn't want to wait till you came home," Dad said.

"What's up?" I asked, feeling a little uncertain after hearing the tone of his voice. He sounded almost too happy. The telephone cord I had been fidgeting with slid out of my fingers.

"Well, two things actually, I got a promotion at work and the family will be moving to Michigan in January and I've asked Jillian to be my wife and she's accepted."

Wow, I wasn't expecting that! I tried to soak it all in as the conversation began to swirl around me. It's odd how life can be turned upside down with a simple sentence.

"So, when is the big day?" Esther asked.

"We were hoping to get married the Saturday after Thanksgiving."

"That doesn't seem like enough time to do that and get the house ready to sell," I said

"Jillian just wants a simple wedding and we will go on our honeymoon in March, once we are settled. That will still give us a month to go through the house."

Esther and I gathered up our pillows, after we hung up and slowly made our way back to our room, feeling stunned and a little unsettled by our dad's announcements.

Michigan was so far away from our home in Utah. Questions raced through my head. What about school? Where would I live? What about Nic?

"Vivian what are we going to do when dad sells the house and moves?" asked Esther.

My thoughts scattered with her question.

"I don't know, I don't think I have enough money saved up to move out. I was planning on living at home still," I said. "You could always go with dad and Jillian. Maybe there is a school out there you could go to."

"That is an idea. I've only been checking into schools closer to home," Esther said.

"It could turn into a grand adventure," I said. "Kind of like this summer."

"Aren't you supposed to meet Nic?" Esther interrupted.

It was 8:45. I jumped up, slipped on my shoes, gave Esther a hug and ran through the open door, right into Nic.

Startled, I asked. "What are you doing here?"

"Got off work early," he said. "What could be a grand adventure?"

"Are you eavesdropping on our conversation Nic?" Esther teased smiling at him as he walked me back into the room.

"I can't help it if I want to be close to your sister," he said as he pulled me against him into a long hug. "Overhearing conversations sort of happen when I'm close. Do you mind?"

"Of course not," I said smiling up at him. I found I smiled a lot when he was around and I was getting to where I liked feeling that happy.

"Our dad is getting married and moving. We're trying to figure out our options," I said.

"I need to think about something else for a while, I'm going to go to the employee lounge and watch a movie," Esther said. "Do you two want to come?"

"No thanks," said Nic. "I think I'd like this pretty girl all to myself for a while if you don't mind."

Esther shook her head and smiled as she tied the laces on her shoes. The three of us walked outside, separating as Esther wandered towards the lounge. Nic took my hand and led me towards the path to the river.

"Not going skinny dipping are we?" I said teasingly. "You know, you tend to lose your clothes when you go down this way."

With that I grabbed the baseball cap off his head and backed away waving it tauntingly.

"You wish," Nic growled a teasing smile on his face. The limp was scarcely noticeable as the space between us diminished.

He slid his arm around me and pulled me tight. His hat kept sliding over my eyes as we continued our walk to the river.

"This will work better," Nic said as he turned it backwards and leaned over for a soft kiss.

The path narrowed and as I strolled in front, our fingers intertwined behind me, images paraded across my mind. The way the wind loved to play with Nic's hair. The intensity that smoldered in his eyes each time he looked at me. His understanding of my fears evoked a deep love for him that only increased after the terror of the fire. His strong hand tightened in mine. We'd been through so much together.

We found a quiet, secluded spot by the river and Nic sat against a nearby log and pulled me down to sit between his legs. Feeling his muscular chest on my back was pure heaven.

"So what are you going to do when your dad and Jillian move?" he asked.

"I'm not sure," I said gazing at the whirlpools in the river. "I guess I will just see if I can find a cheap apartment and a part time job."

"Here's a thought," he said. "What do you think about moving to Colorado and living with me?"

"Live with you?!? I don't know" I stuttered.

"I don't have any roommates and have a nice 2 bedroom apartment."

"Granddad would freak," I muttered.

"Well, what do you think?"

"Do you want me to move in with you?" I questioned.

"Vivian, I wouldn't have asked if I didn't want you there," he said gently tugging on my hair until I looked up at him. "I want you close by all the time."

He leaned over and pressed his lips to mine. Turning without breaking the kiss, I wrapped my arms around his neck.

"I'd love to be with you in Colorado!" I said when Nic's lips left mine.

After a few minutes of basking in the joy of the moment, Nic interrupted. "Oh, I picked up the pictures this morning from our hike. With the fire and all I didn't have a chance to get them earlier."

Sliding off his lap, I snuggled up beside him.

"Have you looked at them yet?"

"No. I haven't had a chance," he said as he reached into his back pocket and pulled them out.

"You bent them!"

Nic just laughed and drew the pictures from the envelope. Slowly going through them, we marveled at the magnificence of the mountains and how high we'd actually hiked.

"What about the mountain lion picture?" I said. "I really want to see that one."

Flipping through the photos we looked for the lion.

"It's not here," Nic said.

"Check again."

We found the picture of us taken by the mysterious woman. The photo I took of Nic and the lion was there as well, except there was no cat.

We looked at each other and then back at the picture, still no lion.

"That's creepy," I said.

"Yeah," said Nic looking back through the pictures. "I'm positive we saw that lion, I don't understand why it's not there," he said thoughtfully.

Sounds of the night seeped into the quiet space Nic and I were in. Birds called out goodnight and were returned by the low rumbled call of a moose. Insects flitted just above the slow moving current.

Sinking further into Nic's side, I murmured, "Wouldn't it be nice if we could just stay right here forever?"

"Well, I've decided to stay here with you until the resort closes."

My lips spread unhurriedly into a smile.

"Only one more week," Rochelle sighed.

We were sitting in the not so crowded cafeteria that morning. The golden brown waffles scarcely touched.

"Why the gloomy faces?" Kenny asked, situating herself lotus style on the chair.

My head ducked beneath the table. Kenny's legs looked like a pretzel. She just shrugged when I sat up. "It's comfortable and I've been practicing."

"We only have one more week and then we won't see each other anymore," Rochelle continued.

"We'll have to make this week count then, won't we?" Kenny responded.

The room was hopping with activity when we entered to begin our shift.

"Good, you are all here," our supervisor Sylvia said. "I know it's a little early, but we need to get to work. There's been a change in the closing date for the resort. I just found out a few hours ago. All patrons will be out by noon today and housekeeping employees will need to vacate their dorms tomorrow by ten."

Frenzied chatter buzzed quietly around the room at the unexpected announcement.

"Get your rooms finished as quickly as you can. There are a few changes in what needs to be done and they're listed on your room assignments."

With a wave goodbye to Rochelle and Kenny I found my cart and went to work.

Leave tomorrow?! I was hoping to have at least one more week with my friends. If I was honest, I didn't want to miss out on the time with Nic. I didn't know when I would see him again. We hadn't made any definite plans about my move to Colorado.

That evening after a dinner of cold cut sandwiches, chips and fruit we descended to our rooms to pack. Strains of Chicago blared through the dorm hall attempting to keep us motivated with its upbeat music.

"Break time," I said, beckoning to Rochelle and Kenny in their room across the hall.

I dropped backwards on my bed. After the long work day and now the frantic packing and cleaning in our room, I was ready to be done.

Esther, Rochelle, Kenny and I crowded onto my bed where we talked, giggled and even cried a little. It was the best, worst night of the summer. I was sure going to miss my new friends.

Morning came quickly and here I was loading my car with a summer full of memories.

"Hey Beautiful," Nic's now familiar arms found their way around me and pulled me close. I set my bag on the seat and turned. My hands moved slowly up his muscular arms and didn't stop until my fingers were lost in his silky hair.

"Hi," I said back.

"This wasn't quite the way I was hoping our goodbye would go," he said quietly.

"Me neither."

"I have to be to work in ten minutes, will you walk with me?" he asked.

I nodded, locked my car and strolled arm in arm with Nic across the parking lot, my head resting on his strong shoulder. We didn't say much just enjoying what little time we had. Nic's goodbye kiss was a mixture of love and heartbreak. I stood there tears running unashamedly down my cheeks as he walked away.

It was strange being back in my old bedroom that I shared with Esther. We had been home for about a week and it was like we fell into a whirlwind. Cleaning out the house was turning into a bigger chore than anyone expected. There's a lot of living that goes on when you've been in a house for over 30 years. So much time was spent sorting, boxing and cleaning. I wondered if it would ever end.

Dad's fiancé, Jillian, ended up being so sweet. I'd been worried about how our family would change with her there, but the more time we had spent together eased my concern.

I needed to finish cleaning out and boxing up the treasures I had buried in my closet, but I found myself staring out the window at the big apple tree. My mind seemed overrun with memories. I could almost taste the apple cider we pressed every fall. Piles of pumpkins lined the edge of the sidewalk waiting to be sold. The hours Esther and I would play hopscotch on the driveway.

"What's the matter, Vivian?" Jillian asked as she stood in my doorway watching me.

"Oh, nothing, why do you ask?"

"You were just staring off into space with a strange look on your face," she said.

"I'm not sure I'm ready to leave all this," I said with a sigh. "I feel like I'm walking away from a lifetime of memories that I can never get back."

"You are leaving a house, Vivian, the memories will go with you," she said. "Why don't you go take some pictures, that way you can have both," she said with just a touch of excitement in her voice.

"Thanks, Jillian, I think I will do just that."

I finished filling the last few boxes and went to get my camera.

"When you're done do you still want to help me find a wedding dress?" Jillian asked when I wandered into the living room trying to decide what pictures to take.

"I've brought over some magazines we can look through," she said.

"That sounds fun, give me an hour and I'm all yours."

The next hour was spent bribing my siblings to pose for me in all of our favorite places. The more pictures I took the better I felt. Scott and Todd made faces in the tree house they had built. Sara in the music room seated at the piano. I even got one of my dad as he sat in his old recliner in the den, stocking feet and all. I took some of mom's flower garden and the old, wooden stool she often sat on in the kitchen. I tried to be deliberate in the pictures that I took. I wanted them to be special.

"I need to remember to thank Nic for his photography help next time I talk to him," I thought as I headed back up to my room.

Jillian and I spent the next hour poring over bridal magazines. There were so many options to choose from when it came to picking a dress. I even found one that I knew had to be mine when I got married. After showing it to Jillian I ripped the page out of the magazine and took it up to my room.

"Vivian," Sara yelled from the bottom of the stairs. "Your boyfriend is on the phone."

Hurrying out of my room, I raced down the stairs, and snatched the phone out of Sara's hand.

"Thanks," I said as I ran back to the privacy of my room, the telephone cord leaving a trail up the stairs.

"How's my beautiful girl today?" Nic asked after I said "Hello."

"Missing you," I responded.

We spent the next while talking about school, my photos of the house and my dad's wedding.

"My dad said I could invite you to the wedding," I said. "It's the Saturday after Thanksgiving so you're invited for Thanksgiving too."

"Will you come?" I asked.

"I'd love to come spend the weekend with you," Nic said. "It will be great to finally meet your family," he added.

After spending about an hour on the phone we said our goodbyes and hung up.

"Talking to Nic I assume," said Esther as she came in our room.

"Yes, I invited him to the wedding and he said he would come," I said a grin plastered to my face.

The bright full moon shone in my window, spreading across my bed. Unable to fall asleep, I laid there staring out the window and thinking about the past few weeks. The wedding was this weekend and Nic would be here tomorrow. I was having second thoughts about moving in with him. All the wedding plans had got me thinking. Would Nic and I get married or just live together? I wasn't sure how I felt about that. I was sure about my feelings for Nic. His face was the last thing I saw as I drifted finally off to sleep.

I hopped out of bed the next morning. Nic would be here today! I thought excitedly.

It was hard to believe that so much time had passed since leaving the resort. The house was getting cleaned out, Thanksgiving was tomorrow and Dad and Jillian would be married by the weekend. I still wasn't positive that moving in with Nic was the best idea for us but I was glad he would be here today so I could talk to him about it.

"Vivian, do you think you could be any louder?" moaned Esther from her bed.

"Sorry, I'm just excited, Nic will be here today," I said as I jumped beside Esther, giving her a good bounce.

"Fine, you go be excited somewhere else and let me sleep," She smiled up at me with tired eyes.

"OK," I said, leaning over and giving her a quick hug before I leaped off the bed and danced my way into our bathroom.

The vantage point from the window seat would allow me to see Nic's car the minute he turned down my street. A book lay unopened in my lap. Jane Austen just couldn't hold my attention that day. I'm sure looking out the window every few seconds didn't help. I set the book aside and rested my head against the cool glass and pulled the fleece blanket up over my shoulder.

It was like I felt more than saw him arrive. I knelt up and looked down the street. Nothing; I started to sink back when I saw something move out of the corner of my eye. Throwing aside the blanket I ran out of the room. His jeep pulled in the moment I made it to the porch. I darted through the thin layer of snow that covered the grass, oblivious to the cold on my bare feet. The hug that met me had never felt better.

My family hovered around us when we finally made it into the house. Introductions were made and I showed Nic to the room he would be staying in.

"Can I have a few moments of your time?" my dad said sticking his head in the doorway.

"Of course, Mr. Lewis."

Winking at me, he followed my dad out of the room. I wandered after them and sat on the stairs, fingering a piece of worn carpet.

"What are you doing?" Jillian asked from the bottom of the stairs.

"Waiting for dad to be done interrogating Nic."

"From what I've seen and what you've told me, I think Nic will be just fine," Jillian said. "I'm headed to the kitchen to finish some centerpieces for tomorrow, you want to help?"

"Can I steal you away for a while?" Nic asked when he finally found me out in the kitchen.

Jillian looked up with a smile, "Go, I'm almost finished here. Thanks for your help."

Setting the ribbons aside, I slid back my chair and stood up.

Walking along the gravel path that led to the gate into the front yard; Nic put his arm around my shoulder and held me close.

"So, what were you and my dad talking about? You were in there for quite a while," I said looking up at him.

"Sex."

"What!"

Nic roared with laughter. "You should see your face?"

I stopped and buried my face in my hands. I could feel the heat of a blush I knew was staining my cheeks.

Nic turned and gently pulled my hands away from my face. Leaning down he gave me a tender kiss.

"Really, that's what we talked about. Your dad was concerned about our living together and he doesn't want me to take advantage of you. He was cleaning his shotgun while we talked. Do I need to be worried about that?"

"Shotgun? How embarrassing," I said. I was a little concerned about that part of our living together, but I just assumed we would talk about it when I got to Colorado.

"He said if he didn't talk to me, your grandfather for sure would."

"I'm sorry about that; my grandparents are really religious and strict in a lot of ways. They tend to butt in a little now that my mom is gone," I said.

"Well, I'm glad I spoke with your dad. It wasn't too bad, just a little awkward," he said with a grin.

Nic was so laid back. I wasn't too surprised to see that that kind of conversation didn't ruffle his feathers in the least. My dad was still going to get an earful tonight, though.

Thanksgiving was wonderful. All the wedding guests weren't arriving until the next day. I was glad to be able to spend the last Thanksgiving in our house with just family and Nic.

"Thanks, for coming this weekend," I told Nic later that night as we were out walking around the neighborhood. "I think my family really likes you."

"What gave that away, don't your brothers wrestle with every boy you bring home?" Nic said chuckling.

I just smiled at him and shook my head.

"Are you still ok with moving in with me next month?" Nic asked me as we walked.

"I was a little concerned a few weeks ago but now that you got 'the talk' from my dad I am really looking forward to it," I said with a grin.

"Were you that concerned about it?" he asked.

"Yeah, but I figured we would talk about it when I got there."

Nic stopped and pulled me into his arms, looking up into his eyes he said, "You know you can talk to me about anything."

I nodded then, putting my arms around his neck, pulled his head down for a long kiss.

Chapter 21

"Dad, did the house sell today?" I asked when I got home from work one afternoon early in December.

"No, their financing fell through but we have someone lined up to look at the house next week."

"I was hoping to be ready to move to Colorado next week," I replied.

"Could you stay a little longer, Jillian had to go out of town for a few days and I could really use your help?" My dad said.

"I guess, I'll call Nic tonight and let him know."

Disappointed, I pulled off my coat, grabbed the phone and dragged it up the stairs to my room. Flopping on the bed, I laid there looking at the ceiling and wondered if I would ever get to Colorado. Once I had made the decision at Thanksgiving to go I was antsy to be on my way. I was hoping to be with Nic by next week.

I sat up and took the pictures off my dresser that Nic had sent. I spread them out on the bed. Some were of him but most of them were photos of his apartment. It was strange they all looked so familiar, like I had been there before.

Two and a half weeks later I was sitting in my now empty room on the phone with Nic again.

"I'm finally leaving," I told Nic. Plans had fallen apart so many times the past few weeks I didn't think I would ever get to Colorado. It was the 23rd of December, weeks after I had hoped to be gone. Most of the things in my room had been shipped to Nic the week before. All I was going to take with me the next morning was my suitcase with clothes that I would need over Christmas. We had decided that we would meet at Nic's parents' house and stay there through the holidays.

Early the next morning, after a tearful goodbye to my family, I got in my car and headed to Colorado. It was a beautiful, sunny, frosty morning. Last week's snow lay in vast piles beside the now dry roads. After a couple hours of driving I pulled over in a remote town to get gas. There was a chilly breeze blowing when I jumped out so I quickly filled up and ran inside to pay. The bright sound of Mannheim Steamroller filled my car as I pulled out and headed towards the highway.

Pulling up to a two story cream colored brick house, hours later, I looked down at the address Nic had given me. I didn't need it however, because glancing up I saw him head out the door and down the sidewalk towards my car. Grinning I leaped out of my car. Running around the front I was caught up in Nic's arms. It felt like I had come home. I wrapped my arms around his neck not wanting to ever let go. The chill in the late afternoon air began to seep under my jacket, as a shiver went through me.

"We'd better get you inside," Nic said "before you freeze."

Nic helped me get my bags out of the car and we hurried in.

"It's nice to finally meet you," Nic's mother said as we walked inside. Coming over she gave me a motherly hug. She was a few inches shorter than me with slightly graying hair.

Stepping back I smiled. "Thank you for having me, ma'am," her blues eyes lit up as she smiled back at me. I could see where Nic got his eyes.

"Please, call me Ruth," she said. "Nic, why don't you take Vivian up to the guest room so she can get settled?"

Grabbing my hand and my bag, Nic led me up the wide curving stairs.

The bedroom was perfect; the walls were a soft pink with a large window on one side, covered with white lace curtains that hung gracefully down to lie puddled on the floor. An antique mirror sat above a light pine dresser which held a beautiful hurricane lamp.

The four poster iron bed was dreamy. I loved the flowing cream colored fabric draped around the top. It reminded me of a bed for a fairy princess.

"There is a bathroom connected to your room and my room is two doors down if you need anything," he said with a smirk as he stepped closer, his arms holding me tight. I looked up anxious for the kiss I knew would be mine. The sounds from downstairs faded as Nic continued to show me just how much he had missed me.

We were both breathing heavily when Nic's lips finally left mine. He looked into my eyes, cupping my still upturned face with his hands. "I think we better go back downstairs if I'm going to keep my promise to your dad," he said grinning. Pressing a quick firm kiss to my lips he stepped back.

Nic's placed his arm around my shoulder and held me snuggly against him. Blushing, I wrapped my arm around his waist and we walked out of the room.

"There you are," a deep voice called as we came into the bright modern looking kitchen.

"Hey dad, I didn't know you were home," Nic said. "This is Vivian. Viv, this is my dad, Arthur."

"Nice to meet you," I said reaching out and shaking his outstretched hand.

"It's a pleasure to finally meet you. You can call me Art," he said with a smile that looked just like Nic's. "Nic has told us a lot about you."

"Nothing too embarrassing," Nic said with a grin lighting up his face.

"Nic could you and Vivian set the table?" his mom asked. "Suppers almost on."

I followed Nic over to the cupboard and took the dishes he handed me. We set them on a small table in the corner.

"No use using the dining room for just the four of us," he said.

"Fine with me," I said. "We don't even have a dining room."

Nic said his younger sister Kristy was spending the night with their older sister, Melissa and would be back the next day; along with his older brother, Michael, his wife Lisa and their young daughter.

After dinner Nic and I went to watch a movie. I really didn't care what we watched, I was just happy to be cuddled up to him with his arm around me.

The kiss was everything a girl dreams of; warm and soft with just a hint of the passion that was to come. Slowly, I came to the realization that it wasn't a dream. I opened my eyes to see Nic bending over me. Catching my eye he leaned back slightly and smiled.

"I was wondering when you were going to wake up."

"What time is it?"

"8:45."

"Get out, get out," I squealed laughing, as I pushed on Nic's shoulders. To no avail, I sunk further into my pillow as he pressed a hard, driven kiss to my mouth.

"Hurry, it's about time for breakfast," he said grinning as he walked out of my room and shut the door.

Throwing back the covers I flew out of bed and scurried into the bathroom. I wanted to make a good impression and sleeping in so late wasn't a good start.

Nic's strong grip stopped me as I rushed out of the bedroom.

"What's your hurry?" he asked.

"You said I was late."

"Everyone else ate hours ago, but I waited," he said just as a timer went off in the kitchen.

"Breakfast is ready," he said smiling at me.

After a hot breakfast of German pancakes, sprinkled with powdered sugar, and a pile of scrambled eggs, Nic took me on a walk around his neighborhood. Just down the street from his house was a small park. Majestic pines towered above the snowdrifts. A large frozen pond was home to the neighborhood boys in a traditional Christmas Eve hockey game.

"I'll have to bring you back when it's gets dark," Nic said, "the trees are all lit up and it looks incredible."

Mundane conversation between Nic's dad and brother floated around the dinner table that evening. I was more interested in watching Nic's adorable niece, eat peas and carrots by the fist full.

I loved Nic's little sister. She reminded me so much of Nic. Her constant smiling all through dinner was contagious. Nic's older sister loved telling stories of Nic when he was little. Of course they were the kind to make even the most confident of men, blush.

"Do you want to go back to the park for a walk?" Nic asked when dinner was done.

Wanting to spend some time alone with him, I readily agreed. Pulling on warm mittens and a knit hat as well as my warmest winter coat, I met Nic at the door.

"I never had the chance to ask you how your goodbyes went with your family," Nic asked as he took my hand and we headed down the sidewalk.

"It was hard but knowing they are leaving in a few weeks as well made it a little easier."

"Are you still ok with sharing an apartment with me?" he asked.

I looked up at him; the look in his eyes told me he really was serious in his question.

Stopping, I took his face in my hands and looked deep into his blue eyes. Illuminated by the street light above us, I said "I love you, Nic. I would live anywhere as long as I could be with you."

Nic responded by wrapping his arms around me and kissing me gently.

"I'm so glad," he whispered when he raised his head.

Taking my hand we headed into the park. It was as amazing as he had said. All the pines seemed to glow, creating a magical wonderland. I didn't pay much attention to where we walked, so mesmerized by the lights and the feel of Nic's hand in mine.

"Look Nic!" I cried, looking up. The sky was full of tiny, shimmering snowflakes. It was like something out of a dream.

Nic and I just stood there watching the falling snow and the twinkling of the lights.

"Viv, I don't think I want you as my roommate."

My heart began to race as I wondered what he meant.

Cradling my face in his hands he stared into my eyes.

"I want you as my wife. I don't ever want us to be apart. Please say you'll marry me?" he said as he reached into his pocket and pulled out the most beautiful ring I had ever seen. It was a simple gold band with an oval diamond encircled by smaller diamonds and emeralds.

The tears that had been gathering began to fall. Nic brushed his thumbs across my cheeks and wiped them away.

"Yes, oh yes." I cried, throwing my arms around his neck.

Nic picked me up, spinning me around and around. The trees, lights and snow disappeared; it was only Nic and I in our own little world.

It was late when we got home. Tiptoeing quietly in the soft glow of the lamp Nic's parents had left on for us, we headed up stairs.

"I guess I better let you get some sleep before Santa gets here," Nic teased pressing a kiss to the tip of my nose.

"I love you," I responded as I backed into my room and quietly shut the door.

I didn't think I would ever get to sleep. All I could think of was Nic holding me in the softly falling snow. I eventually fell asleep as the moonlight slowly moved across the room.

Chapter 22

Christmas dawned cold and clear. I was up early; I never could sleep late on Christmas morning anyway. I could hear giggles as I made my way downstairs. Entering the family room, I saw a tall man who looked so much like Nic that I knew it had to be his brother. Sitting on his lap was the most adorable little girl.

"Morning," he said. "You must be Vivian."

"Yes," I nodded.

"I'm Nic's brother, Michael and this is my daughter, Abbey."

Strong arms snaked around my waist from behind. I hadn't heard Nic come in.

A young woman came in from the kitchen.

"Viv, this is my big sister, Melissa."

Looking over at me with the Ryan smile, she said, "Nice to meet ....You got engaged!" she practically screamed. "When? How? Why didn't you say anything?"

"Slow down sis, we'll tell you all about it when everyone gets here," Nic said calmly.

"What's all the commotion?" Ruth asked as she came bustling in from the kitchen with a petite young woman. Nic took my hand and held it up so his mom and, I soon learned his sister-in-law, could see my ring. Tears filled her eyes as Ruth pulled us both into a tight hug.

"Why is everyone being so loud," a tired voice was heard from the doorway. "I know it's Christmas and all, but still."

"Morning, sis," Nic said. "It's my fault, sorry. Viv said she would marry me and now mom and Melissa can't stop screaming."

"Getting married?" Kristy squealed. She rushed across the room and tackled Nic. It was all he could do to keep us upright. Laughing, he gave his sister a bear hug. I didn't mind being caught in the middle.

"Are we just going to stand around hollering or we going to have some Christmas?" Nic's dad Art's voice boomed from across the room. Smiling, he walked over to us, hugged us tight, and whispered in my ear,

"It's about time someone decided to marry this guy."

I couldn't stop grinning as he pulled away.

The morning was spent passing around gifts and laughing and talking.

"Down to the last package; Kristy could you climb under there and grab that small one in the back?" Art asked his daughter.

"Who's it for?" he continued.

"It's been there for at least a week," Kristy said. "I saw it there. It didn't have a tag, but it does now," she said, waving it around.

Art took the package before it took flight. "It says it's to Nicholas and Vivian Ryan," he said with a puzzled look on his face.

Nic reached up from where we were sitting on the floor and took the small, brightly wrapped package from his dad and handed it to me.

I freed the small box from the red and gold paper. The small silver hinges moved smoothly as I opened the lid. I peered in, curious as to what I would find. Nic's arm brushed mine as he reached over to retrieve the papers and cards that were nestled in the deep blue fabric lining the fancy metal box. As we read through them I could feel the astonishment blossom and burgeon into surprise and then shock.

"Well, what is it?" his mom asked.

"Two airline tickets to Hawaii, an itinerary for a 10 day trip there, hotel and rental car reservations, and a money order made out to Nicholas and Vivian Ryan for $1000..." Nic's voice just faded out at that point.

We just sat there, looking at the papers Nic had spread across the floor in front of us, not quite believing what we were seeing.

"Does it say who it's from?" Lisa asked.

Pulling out a small ornate card sitting in the bottom of the box, I read, "Congratulations on your upcoming marriage. T&E."

Silence hung in the air, questioning looks bounced between us. Who was T&E?

"How about a wedding in Hawaii?" Kristy said holding up the two airline tickets. "I've always wanted to go and I could be your bridesmaid."

I just stared at her as the now familiar scene began to play out in my head; the warm sand, the sunset, a white flowing dress, a tall man standing by the water's edge. His smile and blue eyes were startling in their clarity.

I felt the smile slowly spread across my face as I turned to Nic and said, "Let's do it."

The rest of the day was spent figuring out as many wedding details as we could. Art spent hours on the phone tracking down plane tickets and hotel reservations. When he finally got everything worked out Nic took the phone and we called my dad.

"So, where is this wedding taking place?" my dad asked.

"Hawaii, can you believe it?" I said.

I explained about the mysterious Christmas gift that would allow us to go in two days and have the wedding of my dreams.

"I have nothing to wear," I said sounding like something from junior high. I felt Nic's chest begin to rumble. I tried to glare at him, but couldn't stop the silly grin that radiated the happiness inside.

My dad just laughed and said, "Let Jillian and I take care of that."

"How's that going to work? You are in Utah and I will be in Hawaii."

"Actually, we got this strange card in the mail yesterday from a T&E. You know them?" he said with a chuckle. At that point I started to cry. I just couldn't believe all this was happening.

Nic ended the conversation and held me for a moment. We made our way to the kitchen where his parents were.

"I guess we are headed to Hawaii for a wedding," Nic announced.

The flight to Hawaii was surreal. It was like I was living in a dream. Nic kept laughing at me because I couldn't keep from staring out the window. The water was so beautiful even if there was so much of it.

The islands appeared like tiny specks on a canvas of turquoise.

Our airplane rolled to a stop, we stepped off the plane and I was hit by a humid warmth I found quite different than the dry cold air of Utah and Colorado.

Nic took my hand and we followed the other passengers to the airport from the tarmac. We were greeted by lovely Hawaiian women who placed sweet smelling leis around our necks. Nic even got a kiss on the cheek from one of them. It was fun to see him blush.

We found our rental car, got a map and directions from the rental agency and headed out to have the adventure of our lives. Neither one of our families would be arriving until the next day so we decided to go exploring. Once we checked into our hotel we got our map and headed out. I wanted to see as many waterfalls and gardens as possible. There were so many not too far.

"Let's stop here," Nic said, pulling me out of my revelry and bringing the car to a stop in a small turnout. "There is a trail that leads to a waterfall and springs that we can swim in." Excited to begin our adventure I hopped out, grateful for the swimsuit I had on under my shorts.

The hike was steep for the first mile. We crossed the small stream on slippery rocks to get to the path that continued on the other side. The moist, pungent aroma of the foliage around us filled the air.

We heard the splash of water up ahead and worked our way through the thick vegetation. Plants parted exposing a deserted pond surrounded by lush plants with a 10-15 foot waterfall flowing into it. The concierge at the hotel said this particular waterfall would be fine to jump from because of the depth of the pond. Nic took my hand and we worked our way up the slippery path to the top. Our clothes and towels landed in a heap on a rock. I stared over the edge; it seemed to have grown since we began our climb. It was farther to the pool than I thought. I took a step back and looked at Nic expectantly.

"What, you're not going first?" he asked.

Grinning, I just shook my head.

"How about we jump together," he suggested.

Not giving me a chance to say yes or no, Nic took hold of my hand and we flew off the ledge. My surprised scream pierced the air. Up, up we went. Knowing that going down wasn't optional now; I closed my eyes, took a deep breath and waited to hit the water. I felt Nic's strong grip in my hand and the wind blowing my hair like a fan. The cold startled me as we plunged deep into the water.

I immediately began kicking my way to the top. Air filled my lungs when I broke though the surface. I turned and smiled at Nic. It was scary, but exhilarating at the same time.

"Let's do it again," I said, breathlessly treading water.

Nic nodded and we swam to the edge and climbed out. The trip up to the top was done in record time. I didn't wait for Nic, who had followed me up. I just kept on going until I flew off the edge. Nic was still at the top when I came up.

"What you waiting for?" I called.

Nic smiled, made a loud Tarzan call and threw himself off the falls.

The cannon ball splash threw water everywhere. I kept looking around trying to find him. Fingers wrapped themselves around my ankle and pulled. With a scream I sucked in what air I could and went down into Nic's waiting arms.

He swam us up to the top where we tried to catch our breath. The next hour was spent swimming, jumping and soaking up the sun in a little patch that broke through the canopy of trees that surrounded us.

I felt hungry and a little tired as we gathered our clothes and hiked back to our car. Once we were dry and had our shorts back on we went in search of some real Hawaiian food. We were told about a few places close by. A romantic dinner in a café by the beach was followed by a walk down to the water. Heat from the sand toasted our feet as we ran to the water's edge.

The hotel personnel had been sent some money by T&E for flowers and decorations, and a wedding dinner. I couldn't believe all that we had been given. We still had no idea who had given us this amazing gift.

"You'll meet us one day," I heard a quiet voice say.

"Did you hear that?" I asked Nic.

"Hear what?"

"Oh, nothing," I said.

Probably just another premonition, I thought. I hadn't had many lately, perhaps because I had been so focused on Nic and our wedding.

That evening Nic made us a picnic on the beach. We sat and talked about what we hoped our future would be. Of course we got in some very romantic and heated kisses as well.

"What do you think about having a luau after the wedding? The hotel rep said that could be an option if we wanted it."

"You mean with dancers, a roasted pig and everything?" I asked getting excited by the thought.

"Yes, with all that," Nic said.

"I think that would be a great idea, what do you think?"

"I know our families would love it. It would be a great way to celebrate."

The next day was a flurry of excitement. Our families arrived and getting them settled was a bit of a chore. The younger ones just wanted to play on the beach. Dad said let them have their fun. Who knows if they will ever be here again? Jillian and Ruth had hurried off spending the day in a flutter of excitement. "Wedding plans," they had said. Esther and Kristy spent hours lounging around the pool working on their tans. I got bored and needed some distraction after sitting around with Nic and our dads.

"I'm going to see if Jillian needs any help," I whispered to Nic. He winked and gave me a kiss before I wandered off. I found her unloading the last of the wedding surprises from the rental car. She handed me a small box and a bag from a local grocery store. I followed her back to the room.

"Just set those on the counter and come here. I want to show you something," she said walking back to her bedroom. There on the bed, Jillian had laid out the most beautiful white gown I had ever seen. It was simple in its design, flowing lace with beads sewn randomly throughout. The short sleeves and neckline were edged in small beads. I was anxious to try it on. Stripping down to my underwear and bra, Jillian helped me into it. There were a number of buttons down the back that she quickly did up. She opened the door to the bathroom and turned on the light, as she stepped back I couldn't believe the image that was staring back. I had never felt so beautiful.

"I thought we could leave your hair down and I found these fresh flowers you could wear instead of a veil," Jillian said.

She placed the wreath of white and peach flowers on my head. The green of the leaves were braided and twisted in and around the flowers like an elegant puzzle.

My t-shirt and shorts were a far cry from the dress I had just removed. The wreath sat in its clear plastic container on display in the refrigerator. Through the patios' glass door I could see Nic reclining by the pool.

"Take a walk with me handsome?" I whispered in his ear.

Nic looked up at me. My eyes were drawn to his purely masculine lips. His blue eyes were filled with mischief when I looked into them. He knew I wanted him to kiss me. Heat flooded my face.

"Let's go," he said standing up and taking my hand.

We sat straddled over a large log, my back resting comfortably against Nic's broad chest. The yellow of the setting sun slowly faded to pinks and purples and finally deep dark blue. Waves were making their way leisurely onto the beach. By this time tomorrow I would be married. I sighed in pure contentment and snuggled deeper into Nic's embrace.

"Viv," Nic mumbled into my hair.

"Mmmm," I said.

"Turn around," he breathed in my ear.

I shifted around and found myself sitting in his lap. The light hair on his legs brushed the back of my thighs. Goosebumps skimmed over my legs. Nic gently took my chin in his fingers, tipped my head and brought my mouth up to meet his.

The sand was warm as I stepped onto the beach and began to walk to the water's edge. A blaze of pinks and oranges filled the sky as the sun slowly began to set over the ocean. The lace of my dress brushed the top of my bare feet, exposing the pale pink polish on my toes. I slowly moved towards Nic. He stood so tall and confident, his bare feet sunk in the moist sand. The cream cotton pants hung from his narrow hips. His cream colored jacket stood out against the deep blue of his shirt. He turned to look at me at the same moment a breeze from the ocean tousled his light brown hair. His beautiful blue eyes never left mine as I stepped up next to him. Our forever was about to begin.

The End

<<<>>>

Epilogue

Ryan Estate, East slope of the Colorado Rockies, USA

Sheets the color of freshly cut grass surrounded me as I stretched out in our king size bed. I pulled the ivory colored spread up and snuggled down in its velvety softness. The dark wood trim accented the warm cream color of the walls, creating a perfect backdrop for the painting of an impressive black panther lounging beneath a grove of extraordinary ponderosa pines. Two matching armchairs were arranged in front of the spacious picture window, overlooking the grounds beyond our private garden.

The click of the door and the quiet but distinct sound of footsteps alerted me to Nic's arrival. In the soft peach glow of the crystal salt lamp that sat on a small stand next to our bed, I could see him, so sophisticated in his tuxedo.

Nic had sat down a few feet from me on my oak chest. He slipped out of the shoes I bought him the day he surprised me with dancing lessons then turned and looked at me.

"Hi," he spoke softly when he saw me watching him. "Did I wake you?"

"No, I've been waiting for you to come up," I said softly.

Nic's familiar smile caressed me as he stood and walked across the bedroom to our large walk-in closet.

I lay there silently musing about Nic and our life together as I watched him undress. It had been more than 30 years since I first laid eyes on him in the cafeteria at the mountain resort. He was more muscular and handsome now than when we first met, all those years ago.

The fun we had those two summers. Our amazing wedding on the beach in Hawaii and the first few years in that little two bedroom apartment were glorious. We were so naïve back then. We had no idea what the future held for us. Thoughts of those years came flooding back to me. Nic's illness, the stress and anxiety of just trying to get by; I shook the images from my mind. They were no longer painful but, they didn't bring me joy.

Nic walked barefoot across the lush carpet of our bedroom. He was wearing only his boxers and looked so attractive.

Pictures of today swirled around in my head. The marvelous party Nic had surprised me with filled my heart with an outpouring of love for him. He slid into bed next to me. Before he could reach up and turn off the lamp, I rolled over onto his strong chest. I kissed him long and deep. My tears fell on his cheeks as our lips parted. I could see his smile in the faint glow of the light.

"You okay?" he asked. I kissed him again even longer this time. He returned the kiss without any reservations. When I finally eased back, the tears had slowed a bit, but were still there.

"Thank you," I whispered.

Nic smiled, "Happy birthday, Vivian," he paused gently brushing my hair back off my face. "I hope you enjoyed today."

"I did," I replied. "More than I can say."

He studied my face for a long moment.

"You had another premonition didn't you," he said.

"More like a memory," I responded. "Today, the party, dancing with you, having all of our family and friends around, here at our house, this place, with you;" I paused. "I saw it before."

Nic didn't respond, he just looked at me.

"Years ago before we got married."

He peered deep into my eyes. It felt like he could see into my soul and all the images there.

"After we left that first summer; I saw you. I saw this day. All those years ago; the images weren't clear then, but the emotions were still just as real and intense then as they are now."

Nic smiled and drew me back for a kiss that would last forever.

Acknowledgments

To Brenna Davidson for her help in the creation of this
story.
My appreciation also to Andrew Balls for his creative
abilities in producing the cover design.
To the CVCWC. You all are truly amazing.
A big thank you to Nate Hardy for sharing his gifts and
insights. It is greatly appreciated.
My love and thanks to my amazing husband and family for
their love and support.

About the Authors

Camile R. Rigby found that in writing her first book she very much enjoyed the whole creative process. She loved watching the story come to life.

She lives in the Rocky Mountains of Utah with her husband and family.

Rex Rian is a Success Mentor, Life Coach, Author, and motivational speaker.

You are welcome to contact either of them at www.3peaksinstitute.com or follow them on Instagram at mygoldencopper.